Espionage!

Also from Westphalia Press

westphaliapress.org

Espionage!

by H. R. Berndorff

WESTPHALIA PRESS
An imprint of Policy Studies Organization

Espionage!
All Rights Reserved © 2014 by Policy Studies Organization

Westphalia Press
An imprint of Policy Studies Organization
1527 New Hampshire Ave., NW
Washington, D.C. 20036
info@ipsonet.org

ISBN-13: 978-1-63391-067-6
ISBN-10: 1633910679

Cover design by Taillefer Long at Illuminated Stories:
www.illuminatedstories.com

Daniel Gutierrez-Sandoval, Executive Director
PSO and Westphalia Press

Devin Proctor, Director of Media and Publications
PSO and Westphalia Press

Updated material and comments on this edition
can be found at the Westphalia Press website:
www.westphaliapress.org

Espionage!

by

H. R. Berndorff

Translated by Bernard Miall

New York

D. Appleton and Company

1930

Contents

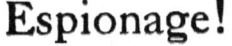

Espionage!

CHAPTER ONE

BEFORE THE WAR

IT is May, 1913. Over the network of the European railways, from Paris, via Warsaw, to Petersburg, from Copenhagen, via Berlin, to Munich, from Amsterdam, via Basle, to Ventimiglia, to and fro, in all directions, the heavy locomotives of the great international railways go roaring upon their way, speeding through the fields and cities and villages of a busy land, in which, as in a single State, men live, love, labour, die, and beget new life. This land is Europe.

The nations of this land are closely bound together by the activities which make them mutually inter-dependent, shaping the individual destinies of all its inhabitants, and giving them all a common likeness. In the cabinets of the governments of these nations problems await solutions which will surely improve the conditions of life for the individual, and guide the struggle for existence of individuals and peoples alike into better and humaner forms. It is the same in Berlin, in London, in Petersburg, in Paris.

The "weekly gazette" of the cinemas, in the last week of this month of May, shows the public of the four great cities: the new international express, a procession of strikers, the latest inventions, the newest airships, aeroplanes, and motor-cars, hewers at work in a coal-mine, the latest giant steamer on the slips, and—to the accompaniment of a blaring orchestra and the applause of the spectators—the march-past of the national troops.

All know the names and faces of the leaders of the armies; and the uniforms, the weapons, the manœuvres of these armies are familiar to the peoples of the great land of Europe. But in Paris, in the rooms of the War Office, the officers of the General Staff are spreading out their great maps, on which their secret plans are so carefully indicated; and their comrades in Petersburg, London and Berlin are poring over similar maps; and in the minds of all these soldiers one question is burning: "What will happen when this state of peace and quiet comes to an end; when the policy of the moment is pursued 'by other means'; when a spark ignites the powder, and a mighty blaze leaps up to the heavens; when this great, peaceful, industrious land of Europe divides itself sharply into nations, and the armies of these nations march to war?

"Let us be prepared for what will happen; above all, let us discover what preparations the enemy has made for war, and what his soldiers are planning; let us learn the secrets of the armies of the nations which may one day be our armed enemies."

So it is in Berlin; so it is in London; so it is in Petersburg; so it is in Paris.

.   .   .   .   .

In May, 1913, a young officer of the General Staff, in uniform, is walking down Unter den Linden. Two older comrades, who, like him, wear the red tabs of the staff officer, pass him with a friendly greeting, and call to him as they pass, "Congratulations!"

The young officer who is thus congratulated is Major Nikolai of the Great General Staff, and he is congratulated because he has just been appointed Chief of the Intelligence Service of the Great General Staff of the German Army. When Major Nikolai takes up his appointment he finds a small intelligence organization which is responsible for the active work of his department, the actual espionage. He has so far only one officer as assistant; his yearly budget is fixed at four hundred and fifty thousand marks, and with this he has to maintain the whole system of defensive espionage. The German secret service is almost devoid of system; it consists, generally speaking, of individuals, of adventurous men and one audacious woman, who are systematically dispatched to the various countries of Europe. In these countries they live, in order to learn their military secrets. The more carefully these few agents are prepared for their task, the more reliable they are. Such men are expressly instructed to investigate secrets of the most important character. The work of these spies is extraordinarily difficult, for France, always distrustful of foreigners in respect of her military affairs, takes the most extraordinary precautions. The secrets of the French Army are so well guarded that the spy cannot hope to attain his object save by a *coup*

de main, a trick, a clever piece of play-acting. It is
very different in Russia; there it has even been possible
to enlist a distinguished officer in the German Intelligence Service, and he, by means of trusted agents, is
able to send important information to Berlin. Among
the civilians on the frontiers many a German spy finds
men and women willing to listen to him, and still more
willing to hold out an eager hand for his German gold.
But in Russia the difficulties are of a different nature.
In such a vast country, where the troops are constantly
being transferred from one garrison to another, and
where there is no uniformity in the matter of technical
equipment, it is impossible to obtain anything more
than individual items of information; as for covering
the whole enormous territory with a network of spies,
there is simply no money available for such a purpose;
an organization of this kind cannot be maintained on a
fraction of four hundred and fifty thousand marks a
year. In respect to France and Russia the German
Intelligence Service confines itself, as a rule, to ascertaining the main aspects of the problem of a military
offensive against Germany. To England a single spy
is sent from time to time. Now, a year before the war,
since England's position in the constellation of the
European Powers is becoming more enigmatical, a few
members of the German Intelligence Service are
stationed there permanently. All communications between the individual spy and the chief of the Intelligence Service of the Great General Staff are made
through a go-between; very rarely does an officer on

4

the active list come into contact with a spy. For the German officer, strangely enough, and quite unjustly, regards the activities of the secret agent with dislike and disdain. In Germany the Great General Staff is busily preparing for war, since war may be inevitable; but one of the most important means of preparation, the organization of espionage, is regarded with abhorrence; and even the new chief of the Intelligence Service, Major (later Colonel) Nikolai, is unable to convert his fellow-officers to a more reasonable way of thinking. He has to make shift as best he can; there is nothing for it but to employ the few trained spies in as many directions as possible, and to prepare them as carefully as may be.

Such is the state of affairs in Germany; but it is otherwise in France.

As long ago as 1894 the German General Staff realized that the French Intelligence Service had succeeded in suborning a considerable number of soldiers in the German Army. Until that year it had had no real knowledge of the extent of French espionage in Germany; but the case of the French commissary, Tomps, proved that the authorities had been under a dangerous illusion. Tomps came from Munich, where his father was a wine-merchant, dealing principally in Bordeaux and Burgundies. After the war of 1871 the father, who, like his son, had retained his French nationality, was sent to Bavaria by the French General Staff, and was so generously treated that he was able to open his wine business in Munich. The fact that the son was constantly travelling to and fro between Munich and Paris attracted no particular attention, since he had, of course, to buy wines and to settle for his purchases. It appeared later, when he was detected, that the French General Staff had had him specially trained for his work in Paris, and at the instance of the General Staff the International Wagons-Lits employed the young man in the capacity of inspector. In the cars of the Wagons-Lits he travelled all over Germany. At the same time, however—and it was this that led to his detection—he was entered on the roll of the French police as "Special Commissary for Defensive Espionage." As a matter of fact, his work had nothing whatever to do with "defence." It was ordinary espionage of the most wholesale description, and of a peculiarly cunning character. The smart young inspector had in Munich a host of "lady friends," whom he paid most generously, and who were entirely devoted to him. These girls—little dancers, chorus-girls and dramatic students—young women of small talent, but of catholic affections—he sent all over Germany, and took half a dozen of them to Berlin. These women agents, to whom Tomps paid a generous monthly wage, were given the task of making up to young officers, more especially to officers of the technical troops, in order to learn from these men as much as they could be induced to tell. In Berlin two of these girls contrived to attach themselves to two young officers of the School of Artillery. In both these cases they proceeded with extraordinary skill. They began

6

by inducing the two young officers to spend more than they could afford; they then introduced them to a circle of gamblers; and when the two young men were in such financial straits that they did not know where to turn, and had already resorted to means of procuring money which would have led, on their exposure, to disgrace and dismissal from the service, a mysterious person, whose name was never mentioned, made his appearance, and offered them a very large sum of money if they would obtain certain documents from the School of Artillery and the School of Engineers. The two young men did what was required of them: they not only stole such documents as were accessible to them, but they photographed the models of the latest and most secret engines of war. The discovery of these thefts enlightened the German Intelligence Service as to the true state of affairs. Quietly the Department devised its measures of defence, and set to work to uncover the trail of the French secret agents. It soon made the most alarming discoveries. It appeared that the French Intelligence Service did not always work from Paris, as it had done in the case of Tomps, but that it had its chief offices, with permanent organizations working under them, in countries which, it was presumed, would remain neutral in the event of war. In Geneva, for example, there was Lieutenant-Colonel Parschet, with no less than ninety subordinates. To all appearances the office was that of a mercantile firm, and its employés travelled all over Germany—but only in order to pursue their trade of espionage. The firm had a branch office in Basle, whose business it was to keep the Bavarian Army under observation. Smaller firms, with fewer employés, were established in many of the Dutch towns also, whose real business it was to undertake espionage in Germany. But it is only to-day, more than ten years after the end of the war, that we have realized that the French Intelligence Service had established itself firmly, long before the war, in the very heart of Germany. It did not, like the German Intelligence Service, make shift with a few individual spies, dispatched now to one country and now to another, but maintained, in the great German cities, permanent agents who entered the service for life. These agents almost invariably went to work in the same manner: they instructed women to make advances to young German officers, and in some cases these methods were successful. There was, for example, the artillery lieutenant, Helmuth Wessel, from Minden in Westphalia, who was introduced, by a French agent in Cologne, to a young "Frenchwoman," who had as a matter of fact enjoyed a brief celebrity at the time of the Dreyfus trial—"Mademoiselle M.B.," whose full name, as we know to-day, was Mathilde Bäumler, and who was no Frenchwoman, but a native of Charlottenburg. Wessel, who fell a victim to this woman, fled the country when his crime was discovered, but was extradited, and after a trial which was a *cause célèbre*, and which, after opening in Thorn, was transferred to Berlin, he was sentenced to a term of imprisonment. After his release he married the woman who had ruined him and settled down with her at Nice. Here he continued to work for the French Intelligence Service; his beautiful wife had to make the acquaintance of German officers in Nice, accompany them to Monte Carlo, and induce them to play at the tables. The officer, of course, always lost, and as his helper in need, according to the time-honoured formula, the mysterious stranger intervened; played in this case by Herr Wessel, the cashiered officer, who offered large sums of money for the betrayal of military secrets.

The cases in which French spies were successful in obtaining information in pre-war Germany were literally beyond computation. All that we know is the number of the cases in which enemy spies were actually arrested and brought before a German court. In the year 1913 alone three hundred and forty-six persons were arrested on charges of espionage. They were almost all working for France, and it says much for the skill with which these agents went about their business that only in twenty-one cases was there sufficient evidence to procure a condemnation. The French authorities received much useful information from German deserters who fled over the frontier, and from men who, having served in the German Army, sought to enlist in the Foreign Legion. Certain officers of the French Army were specially appointed to question such renegades. The whole French Intelligence Service in Germany was most brilliantly organized, and its principal agents were men whom even the great Fouché (who, though he lived a hundred years ago, has always

9

been regarded as the greatest master of espionage and the methods of the secret police) would have distinguished by his praise.

Such were the French methods; the English were very similar.

The headquarters of the British espionage in Germany was, like the French headquarters, in a neutral country: in Belgium. Captain Renguart, a staff officer, had his office in Brussels, at No. 7 Rue Garchard. A number of English officers, mostly engineers or gunners, were temporarily attached to the service. This British bureau worked hand in hand with the French Intelligence Bureau in Amsterdam, where the British themselves had a branch of their Brussels office. With the practical genius of their nation, the English, after long preparation, accomplished a piece of espionage unexampled in the history of the pre-war secret services. They placed agents in the great cities of the Rhine, extending from Holland to Switzerland, and in the German cities on the route Amsterdam-Hanover-Schneidemühl-Thorn. Along this route they flew carrier-pigeons, by means of which they could at any time, even in serious emergencies, forward news and information. Early in the year 1914 this organization was perfected in the most ingenious fashion. The British secret service agents had noted that the carrier-pigeons followed, in the one case, the course of the Rhine, and in the other the railway between Amsterdam and Thorn. They now had tiny cameras made, so light that they could be fastened to the birds' tails. These appliances were fitted with clockwork, which at set times would expose portions of a film, and since a whole flight of pigeons was always released simultaneously, and their cameras could be set to make exposures at different times, it would be possible to obtain a fairly continuous series of photographs. The pictures were of course very minute, but could be enlarged at will. For times of peace this organization was useless; but in time of war it might have been of enormous value, as it would give information of movements of troops and material.

The permanent English agents in Germany were not quite so numerous as the French. They worked, if possible, in a more brutal fashion than their French colleagues. They were responsible for burglarious entries into the quarters of German naval officers, just as the French agents broke into quarters of the frontier officers in Alsace-Lorraine. But the greatest achievement of the British Intelligence Service was the affair of Wilhelmshaven. The British, of course, were chiefly interested in spying out the secrets of the German coastal defences, and they actually contrived for some years to maintain an intelligence bureau in Wilhelmshaven itself. It was installed in a villa, and as a precaution against sudden surprise this isolated villa was provided with an underground passage. The British agents succeeded in corrupting two Wilhelmshaven policemen and a signalman's mate, with the result that the German authorities had to transfer or dismiss almost the entire police-force of the port. The most famous English spy ever to operate in Germany was an English officer on the active list (later to become Lord Baden-Powell—the founder of the Boy Scout movement), who travelled all over Germany. Lord Baden-Powell, who even to-day is considered an authority on espionage, sent his superior officers in London certain reports which he subsequently published, and which were at the time regarded seriously. The substance of one of his reports is reproduced as a curiosity:

"As in Belgium (he says), so in France, the Germans examine the whole of the country which would presumably be the scene of battle in the event of hostilities. Where they note favourable positions for their artillery they are already (in peace-time, before the year 1914) laying the necessary foundations and preparing their gun-emplacements. In order that no suspicion may be aroused, a German buys or rents the land chosen for the gun-emplacements, has the ground marked out for a farm building—or, if there is a town in the neighbourhood, for a factory—and even erects a light building on the spot."

This method of selecting the positions for the artillery years before the date of an imaginary battle in enemy territory, on which, as a matter of course, hostilities would at first assume the form of an open war of manœuvre, is one that the worthy peer should patent. The very idea is grotesque—but Lord Baden-Powell asserts that he himself saw such German gun-emplacements both in France and in Belgium, and this in a time of the profoundest peace.

But England had men at her disposal who were less ready to jump at conclusions. The majority of her spies were men of extraordinary ability, who in many cases made their way into the very strongholds of the German sea-power, to Kiel Harbour and the Kiel Canal, and remained there undetected for considerable periods. The British officers Brander and Trench, and an English lawyer, Stewart, were arrested by the German authorities, shortly before the war, while engaged in such an undertaking. But in almost all cases, and always in matters of great importance, the individual English spies, who were generously paid by their Government, used to work in co-operation with their French colleagues, so that London was constantly in receipt of reports from the central agency in Brussels, which kept it well informed as to the state of the German armaments.

So much for the British methods: the Russians went to work in quite a different manner.

The actual headquarters of the Russian secret service was in Warsaw; the head of the service was the General Staff officer Batjuschin, who had to send out his spies in two directions, into Germany and into Austria. He, of course, unlike his French and British colleagues, was concerned principally with the strength of the military forces on the German frontier. Having almost unlimited means at his disposal, he was able, by means of wholesale corruption, to induce innumerable German

and Austrian citizens to undertake acts of espionage in
the frontier districts. He had in his pay an enormous
number of small tradesmen, who, in pursuit of their
ordinary affairs, were constantly crossing the frontier,
and his efforts were ably seconded by the officers of the
Russian Army who were stationed on the German frontier, and who, by tradition, were inoculated with the
idea that active espionage was an essential part of their
duties. Whole armies of Russian agents penetrated
far behind the German frontier, and promptly reported
the slightest alteration in the disposal of the German
forces. But wholesale as these measures were, they
failed entirely to achieve their object. Even in matters
of espionage too many cooks are apt to spoil the broth,
and these people in the pay of Russia were almost all
ignorant of military affairs, so that although the central
agency in Warsaw certainly learnt a great deal, most of
the information which it received was of no real value,
or positively false. Not until shortly before the war did
the Russian Intelligence Service adopt other methods.
Ceasing to rely on Russian agents in Germany, it confined itself to corrupting men and officers of the German
Army. A regimental clerk in the fortress of Thorn,
who was personally visited by Batjuschin in his garrison, photographed the plans of the fortress and delivered them to the Russian. A regimental clerk in the
fortress of Breslau, likewise after a personal interview
with Batjuschin, did the same thing. Both men were
detected and confined to long terms of imprisonment.
On the whole, however, the Russian Intelligence

Service, which was by no means equal to the English service, to say nothing of the French, had little success in Germany; so little, indeed, that at the beginning of the year 1914 it suddenly decided to instruct the Russian Military Attaché in Berlin, Colonel von Basarov, despite his official position, to take an active part in the work of espionage. Basarov was at first successful. From disloyal non-commissioned officers he was able to buy the plans of almost all the German fortresses on the eastern frontier. The German General Staff, however, was informed of his activities by a Russian officer of high rank who was acting as a spy in the pay of Germany. The messenger who was to have taken the plans to St. Petersburg was at the last moment arrested on board a German vessel, and the Military Attaché hastily packed his boxes and returned to Russia.

The Russian Intelligence Service was more successful in Austria than in Germany. In the latter country it had not been able to corrupt any officer in a really responsible position, but in Austria it succeeded in doing so. There were other reasons, too, for its greater success in Austria. In view of the political constellation of Europe, war between Russia and Austria seemed more immediately probable than war between Russia and Germany. The Austrian frontier was not flooded by a regular invasion of spies as was the German frontier, but individual Russian spies, men of military training with a knowledge of military affairs, travelled about the country. These agents acquired information of great value.

ESPIONAGE!

It may be said, as a general thing, that wholesale espionage gives poor results, while the specially qualified individual spy succeeds in doing work of real value. The explanation of this fact is psychological. As in war, as in every kind of mutual conflict, as in the economic competition of one country with another, as in cases where large commercial undertakings with many branches come into conflict with individuals, it is never the organization which is victorious, but always the individual, the man with courage and with new ideas. The methods of mass espionage, the questioning of deserters and so forth, are merely an element of military technique; they have their laws and their limits. These, like all technical details, are quite without interest for the uninitiated. The reason why there is such a general interest in espionage, why it is always, and not without reason, regarded as a romantic subject, is to be found in the individual exploits of those spies, whether men or women, who venture into foreign countries in order to discover their secrets. These pages record the history of such exploits.

CHAPTER TWO

POLICEMEN AS SPIES

WILHELMSHAVEN is by no means an in-
spiring place at the best of times; least of
all when the town, which existed, before the
war, only for the service of the harbour, is seen under
a downpour of rain. If you were to enter the town by
night, when hardly a soul is to be seen in the dimly
lighted streets, apart from a few sailors hurrying back
to their barracks through the drenching rain, you would
find it difficult to imagine that anyone could of his own
free will spend the greater part of his life in Wilhelmshaven. Some such thought, no doubt, was in the mind
of a certain man who, on a wet summer night in the
year 1910, was standing on the outskirts of the town,
before the fence of a garden, in which a small house
could be seen through the trees and bushes. The house
was in a lonely position, surrounded by fields and gardens; its nearest neighbour, a larger villa, which also
stood in a spacious garden, was some two hundred yards
distant. The man who was standing before the garden
fence had ascertained, some weeks earlier, that quite a
number of persons appeared to be living in the small
villa. They were persons of both sexes, who were unusually well dressed; and he had particularly noted

that they wore very valuable rings on their fingers; in short, they must be wealthy people. But to-night they were not at home. The watcher had seen three men and a woman leave the house, enveloped in capacious waterproofs, and he had ascertained, having watched the house for days, that for the moment only these three men and this one woman were living in the villa.

Choosing a particularly dark spot on the road, which was dimly lit only by a very distant street-lamp, the man went up to the garden fence. There was a sudden harsh click; with a pair of cutting-pliers he had severed a strand of barbed wire. A wriggle and a jump landed him on the wet soil of a flower-bed. Then, keeping to the grass as far as possible, he approached the house. It was dark and silent, and dripping with rain. All the shutters were closed. Only at the back of the house, in the gable, a small window was open, and here was a lean-to shed whose roof reached some distance up the wall of the house.

The man went up to the shed. He drew the leather belt of his waterproof tighter round his body, climbed on to a water-butt, got a grip of the branches of an es-palier fruit-tree, and managed to scramble on to the roof of the shed. The open window was about nine feet above him. He felt along the wall, found a purchase for his hands, pulled himself up on to a mould-ing, and suddenly swung himself in through the window.

He found himself in absolute darkness. He could feel that he was standing on a soft carpet. He took a flash-lamp from his pocket, but even as he pressed the button, and the light fell on the white door of the room, he received such a blow on the head that he fell to the floor unconscious.

The house, the garden and the street were now more silent than ever. Only at the end of the street, which ran between gardens and a few isolated houses, firm footsteps were audible. A policeman, his collar turned up about his ears, his hands in his pockets, with the rain dripping from his helmet, was slowly going his rounds.

When the man who had climbed through the window of the villa recovered consciousness he was lying on the floor of a bedroom. He opened his eyes; there before him was a tall, strongly-built woman, sitting in an arm-chair and smoking a cigarette. He tried to stand up, and found that his hands and feet were tied. He was lying, apparently, in the woman's bedroom. He looked at the woman in dismay, and this dismay became terror when he saw that she had taken his letter-case from his pocket as he lay unconscious, and was now examining its contents. When the woman saw that her prisoner had recovered consciousness she addressed him as follows:

"The photograph I find here is very like you, Herr Glauss, but I must confess the policeman's uniform suits you better than the shabby waterproof you are wearing now. You have still a very great deal to learn, Herr Glauss. I have noticed for days how you have been hanging round our little house, and I saw you creeping across the garden. I was standing at the window as you climbed the wall, and I knocked you out as you entered the room. I wouldn't hesitate to knock you unconscious again, and throw you out of the window, where you would probably break your neck. And I certainly shall do so if you don't tell me who sent you here. I see from your papers that you are a sergeant of the Wilhelmshaven police; and I have never heard that the Wilhelmshaven policemen are in the habit of climbing through attic windows. So—who sent you, and what do you want in this house?"

"No one sent me," said the man, who saw that the game was up. "I was only going to break into the house because I am in need of money. If you give me up I am a ruined man. Let me go, and I promise to live an honest life in future."

The woman laughed. She flicked the ashes of her cigarette on to the man's face, and said:

"You expect me to believe that? It is only by chance that you picked upon this house? You are simply an ordinary burglar, nothing more? Do you seriously want me to believe that?"

The prisoner did not understand his captor. After more than an hour's inquisition, during which she untied the sergeant and gave him a chair, the woman was finally convinced that Glauss was really a policeman, who had got into trouble, and had actually broken into the house merely in the hope of stealing money or valuables.

Being at last convinced of this, she considered a while. In the meantime doors were opened and closed in the house below; the other inmates had apparently returned. Finally she surrendered to the man's pleading, and the burglar left the house as he had entered it, by the window.

He ran as though pursued across the garden, jumped over the fence, and hurried along the street. He did not see that two men who had run out of the front door of the house were following him, swiftly and with infinite dexterity, along the fence of the gardens and allotments. When Glauss had run a considerable distance he stopped suddenly, exhausted, and leaned against a tree. One of his mysterious pursuers was at this moment only some twenty yards behind him. Then footsteps were heard in the distance, and once more a policeman in full uniform came slowly down the street. Glauss raised his head. As the officer came into the light of the street-lamp Glauss suddenly gave a peculiar whistle. The policeman hastened his steps, and approached him. Thereupon the man who was pursuing the burglar leaped silently over the ditch; in a flash, and without a sound, he was over the wooden fence; he ran cautiously forward, and crouched behind the fence close to the tree against which Glauss was leaning. The policeman had now come up to Glauss. And this is what the hidden listener heard:

THE POLICEMAN: "What happened to you?"

GLAUSS: "Don't ask me. As I was climbing through the window a woman knocked me senseless. My head is still buzzing. She took my papers out of my pocket; she knows who I am."

THE POLICEMAN: "Good God, is she going to denounce you?"

GLAUSS: "I don't think so; but the most important thing is, where are we going to get money before to-morrow morning? You know they audit the district accounts to-morrow."

The listener gathered from this and from their further conversation that the two men, Glauss and Jaenicke, both of the Wilhelmshaven police force, were in great financial difficulties, which had been further aggravated by the embezzlement of sums from a fund for which they were responsible. He learned, moreover, that the speakers had committed a number of burglaries together, and that Glauss proposed that very night to break into the office of a brewery in the neighbourhood, after Jaenicke, in full uniform, had carefully reconnoitred the position.

This burglary was actually perpetrated that night by Glauss and Jaenicke. They succeeded in laying their hands on several hundred marks, but they were watched all the time by two men who had secretly and adroitly followed them.

About a week later, one Saturday evening, the two policemen, in full uniform, came down the road in which the lonely villa stood. They were walking together, in accordance with the police regulations of the garrison town, for on Saturdays it sometimes happened that drunken sailors were guilty of "disorderly conduct" or "causing a breach of the peace." They patrolled the road, as prescribed, from end to end, and as they were returning a tall, broad-shouldered man suddenly emerged from the house of which Glauss had such unhappy recollections. Waiting until the two policemen had come up to him, he accosted them thus:

"Gentlemen, I think it would be as well if you were to come into the house with me."

Jaenicke, who, it will be remembered, knew all about his friend's unsuccessful attempt at burglary, felt very insecure, and tried to conceal his embarrassment by adopting a blustering official tone:

"What do you want us there for? Have you anything to report?"

The tall man laughed, and said:

"All sorts of things. I should like to give you the names and addresses of the men who committed a certain burglary in the offices of a brewery. It's an affair that has interested me enormously. And, of course, it was reported in the papers."

Glauss turned pale.

Jaenicke, however, who still had hopes of a harmless *dénouement*, continued to play his part as a policeman: he thrust his hand into the breast of his tunic, brought out his notebook, took his pencil, and said:

"If you know the perpetrators it is your duty to denounce them. Give me their names!"

Then the stranger looked very serious. He gave Jaenicke a searching look, and proceeded:

"Please note the names! The men who committed the burglary were: a sergeant of the Wilhelmshaven police, Glauss, and his comrade, Sergeant Jaenicke."

The two policemen were silent. The hand in which Jaenicke was holding his notebook fell to his side. And the stranger continued:

"But we can talk the matter over, of course, if you find the subject a painful one. Come into the house."

He preceded them through the garden; the two policemen followed him, obediently, into a large, well-furnished sitting-room on the ground floor of the villa.

In this room sat a woman. She was reading a book. She nodded curtly. Glauss knew her only too well; it was she who had received him in the attic on the night of his burglarious entry.

The man who had stopped them in the road offered the two policemen chairs, poured out a couple of glasses of beer, gave them cigars, and waited until his bewildered guests had lit them. Then he spoke:

"I will begin by telling you who I am. I am an engineer, Petersen by name, and this lady is my sister. You will not find us on the police register; on our passports it is stated that we are only passing through the country. I tell you this so that you may not be surprised if you should look up our names and fail to find them. In a fortnight or so we shall be gone for good. My sister, Herr Glauss, told me that you had tried to break into the house. I followed you, and I heard what you said when you met your comrade in the road. I knew, from what you said then, what burglaries the two of you have committed during the last few weeks. What I know would be enough to send you both to prison for some little time."

24

Glauss had collapsed in his chair. He covered his eyes with his hand; he seemed bewildered. But Jaenicke, at Petersen's concluding words, sprang to his feet. His face was flushed, and he swayed a little as he stood.

"How dare you say so!" he shouted. "I know nothing of Glauss's breaking into your house. We were simply speaking of burglaries down the road because we were looking for the burglars! You misunderstood the whole conversation! What's that you say—that we broke into the office of the brewery? Libelling the police is a serious offence, my good sir!"

Petersen, who was standing beside him, laid his hand on the policeman's shoulder, and said:

"Very well, if you like I will go to the telephone and call the criminal police. But I warn you," he continued, softly, in a voice that was almost a hiss, "when I denounce you I shall give the authorities this photograph."

He took a photograph from his pocket and passed it to Jaenicke, who involuntarily held out his hand for it. It was a night-exposure. It showed the courtyard in which lay the office of the brewery which had lately been broken into. Two men appeared in the photograph, who were plainly recognizable: they were Glauss, in mufti, and Jaenicke in uniform. Glauss was climbing out of a window, and Jaenicke was helping him down. The moonlight was falling on them both; it had rained all the rest of the night, but for a few moments the moon had appeared from behind the clouds.

"An excellent camera, isn't it?" whispered Petersen.

Jaenicke threw the picture on the floor; he himself dropped into an easy-chair, and stared into the face of the man who stood smiling before him.

It was well into the small hours when the two policemen left the house. Petersen had promised them that their crime should not be denounced; each of them had in his pocket an advance of five thousand marks, and they had undertaken to accomplish a task of whose dangers and consequences they preferred not to think.

On the following day, which was a Sunday, Jaenicke, in civilian clothes, entered the pinnace of the *Von der Tann* and went on board the cruiser. He had a day's leave, and he wanted to persuade his friend, the signalman, Ehlers, to come ashore with him and spend the evening in a tavern. Ehlers and he were acquaintances of many years' standing; in a sense, indeed, they were almost connections, for Ehlers was engaged to Jaenicke's sister-in-law. The only reason why the lovers were not already married was that they had not sufficient money. Before Jaenicke went off to the cruiser he had visited his sister-in-law, and had a long conversation with her. That evening the three met in the town. Ehlers and his fiancée were agreeably astonished when Jaenicke informed them that he had bought three tickets for a variety show, and they were still more surprised when after the performance the policeman invited them to a restaurant which was known to them, only by name, as both fashionable and expensive. Here Jaenicke ordered food and wine; and suddenly Glauss appeared in his best civilian clothes, and sat down to table with

them. It was not long before Jaenicke mentioned the
fact that his sister-in-law was anxious to get married at
once, and later, when the cork flew out of their first
bottle of champagne, he passed his friend, the signalman, a thousand-mark note, and suggested that there
was now no reason why he should not get married.
The marine opened his eyes at this, for he knew well
enough that Jaenicke never had a penny to bless himself
with, so that his sudden generosity was rather mysterious. But the wine had already done its work. He was
no longer capable of logical thought; he put the note
away and continued to drink. From that day onwards
Jaenicke was constantly bringing him ashore whenever
he was off duty. Sooner or later the two friends invariably disappeared into some tavern, and there they
were always joined by Glauss. At first the marine
racked his brains to discover where the two policemen
got all their money; but he used the thousand marks to
buy furniture; his fiancée rented a flat, and made
numerous purchases, giving the bills to Ehlers, who
was expected to settle them out of the thousand-mark
note. Before he had realized what he was doing,
Ehlers was three thousand marks in debt. A few days
later, being once more in his cups, he told his troubles
to his friends, the policemen. In the daytime, as he
went soberly about the decks of the cruiser, the whole
affair seemed like a bad dream. How on earth was he
to get the money to pay the debts his fiancée had in-
curred? He could not understand what had induced
his future wife, who had always been such a modest,

sensible sort of girl, suddenly to insist on buying a whole houseful of things which she would probably never be able to pay for. That evening, however, when Jaenicke and Glauss dragged him almost by force from tavern to tavern, and the drink was beginning to cloud his brain, he once more saw things in the rosiest of colours. To his many inquiries as to how Jaenicke and Glauss had come by the money which had enabled them to enter upon such a course of riotous living, he received always the same reply: that Jaenicke had inherited some money, and that there was still more to come.

That evening, as he despairingly confessed to his debts, and declared that he did not know where to turn, Jaenicke was full of good advice. But he gave the sailor more than mere advice: he went so far as to promise him that he would pay the debts out of his inheritance. He could not lay his hands on the amount at the moment, but there was a man who had something to do with the paying over of the legacy, and Jaenicke would get the money out of him. By the following day the whole affair would be settled. That night, as Ehlers staggered on board the cruiser, he was perfectly happy, though rather drunker than usual.

At the little villa on the outskirts of the town all seemed as usual as the weeks went by, except that every morning, about daybreak, the two policemen, Glauss and Jaenicke, might have been seen to enter the house. They were loyally performing what they had pledged themselves to do in return for money and the promise of silence in respect of their burglaries. Glauss had made the acquaintance of one of the men employed at the waterworks; he had often gone out with him, and had told him, incidentally, that an engineer had asked him whether he could one day obtain the plans of the water-mains of the town, and also the plans of the individual pumping-stations. This appeared to be quite a harmless request, for the engineer had invented some sort of machinery by which the necessary pressure in the mains could be obtained at very much less than the usual cost. He was anxious to offer his invention to the town of Wilhelmshaven, and he wanted to have a look at the plans of the waterworks, so that he might be prepared to answer any questions which the municipal authorities might put to him. The waterworks employé declared immediately that the thing could not be done. The plans were absolutely secret; since the place was a naval port, they were very important, and it was quite impossible to inspect them.

"A pity!" said Glauss. "The man promised me two thousand marks if he could see them only for half an hour. I would have given you a thousand."

For a subordinate official of a municipal waterworks a thousand marks is a considerable sum of money. Half an hour is only a short space of time; nothing much can happen in half an hour. And one evening the employé took the plans of the waterworks from the safe in which they were kept, and, hiding them under his coat, took them to Glauss, who was waiting in the road outside. The policeman took them to a house standing in a garden in a lonely road on the outskirts of the town. Ten minutes later he returned, and said: "Here are the things, and here is a thousand-mark note. The engineer can't do anything now about the plans; he has already sold the patent elsewhere; but he has given me the money all the same. He is a decent sort of fellow." The municipal employé put the note in his pocket, ran back with the precious plans, explained to the door-keeper that he had forgotten something, and returned the plans to the safe, after convincing himself that none were missing.

On the following day the policeman, Glauss, went on leave. He said good-bye to his comrades, informing them that he was going to spend his holidays with a married sister in Hamburg.

He went to Hamburg wearing a coarse waterproof cape, which he had had by him for some years, a suit which was already shiny at the knees and elbows, and thick woollen stockings. Glauss was a married man, but his marriage was not a happy one. He was not divorced, but his wife lived with her parents. When he arrived in Hamburg he disappeared in the crowd, hurrying out of the terminus into the streets of the great city.

That evening a gentleman, dressed in extremely smart and rather conspicuous clothes, whose luggage consisted of two brand-new leather trunks, went to the tourist office of the railway station and bought a first-class sleeping-car ticket for Paris. This gentleman was the Wilhelmshaven policeman, Glauss, whose only object in going to Paris was to have a thoroughly good time. The bars and dance-halls of Montmartre were patronized in those days by a visitor who threw his money about in such a reckless fashion that the waiters and *les filles* took him for a land-agent who had run away with the year's revenue, or for a factory porter or bank messenger who had stolen the money entrusted to him. But that did not prevent their quickly and gracefully relieving the German of his wealth. In this they were ably assisted by one Mademoiselle Yvonne, aged twenty-two, a native of Marseilles, who became very intimate with our *viveur*.

Jaenicke, however, remained in Wilhelmshaven, waiting until his leave was due. But before he went on leave his paymaster required him to complete his transactions with the signalman's mate, Ehlers. Jaenicke accordingly continued to play his part. One day he gave Ehlers the three thousand marks wherewith he was to pay his debts. The money had been provided by the man who had "something to do with paying over the legacy." All he wanted was a receipt, which the marine wrote on a long strip of paper. The lines were not very straight, nor the signature very steady, for Ehlers was asked to sign the receipt when he was already very drunk.

Now matters proceeded quickly. Ehlers' new house was furnished and ready; the wedding was to take place in perhaps two months' time. The marine was already living in the midst of his new splendour during his hours on shore, when one day a man knocked on the door of his Paradise, and held before the eyes of the astonished inmate a promissory note for more than three thousand marks, with a polite request that it should be paid then and there, as it had fallen due.

Ehlers fell from the clouds. When he heard the words "promissory note" he realized what had happened. And the man who had produced the note gave him a short but highly instructive little lecture, from which he gathered that his new furniture, of which the whole neighbourhood was envious, would be removed by the officers of the court.

"But did you never consider how you were going to pay this sum?" asked his caller.

"No," said the marine, frankly, in a tone that carried conviction.

The holder of the note—a tall, broad-shouldered man of good appearance—raised his eyebrows.

"But that is going too far!" he said. "Then you have committed a forgery which is punishable with imprisonment!"

The marine was terrified. He had little general education; he did not realize the absurdity of the statement; he heard only the words "forgery" and "prison," and he thought that the stranger was probably speaking the truth. The dim feeling that there was something queer about his good luck had never left him, though he had done his best to drown it in alcohol.

The stranger sat down in an arm-chair and explained that he had bought the note from a business man with whom he was slightly acquainted, only because the policeman, Glauss, who was a personal friend of his, and of whose integrity he had a high opinion, had assured him that Ehlers was a man to be trusted. As a matter of fact, he was not in any urgent need of the three thousand marks, since he was quite comfortably off; still, after all, he must somehow get his money back. But he had quite forgotten to introduce himself: his name was Petersen; he was an engineer by profession; and he was making only a short stay in Wilhelmshaven.

"Well," he continued, "all this is beside the point! I suppose you won't mind if I have a look at your furniture, and so forth, to judge whether it is worth the money. Of course, you know, second-hand things don't fetch much of a price: but I am not really worrying about that, for after all I can always raise money on the security of your pay."

As the marine, pale and despairing, showed the engineer over his dwelling, he told himself that he would never survive the misery of seeing his home ransacked by the bailiff and of knowing that his pay was hypothecated. How ashamed he would feel when he had to tell the neighbours, and his fiancée, and her parents, what had happened!

Petersen was standing at the window, looking out into the street. Ehlers was brooding in silence. Suddenly Petersen cried: "Oh, just open the window, there is Glauss down there; we will ask him to come up for a moment."

As chance would have it, at this very moment the policeman looked up at the window. He was in uniform, and to all appearances was patrolling his beat.

The engineer beckoned to him from the window; Glauss crossed the street, and presently he was standing in the sitting-room of the unfortunate marine.

"Well, Herr Glauss," said the engineer, "this is a nice business you've let me in for! You told me Herr Ehlers was such a respectable man, and now he stands there and tells me he cannot pay this note."

Glauss, who had been recalled from Paris by a mysterious telegram, and had at once resumed duty, meaning to take the rest of his leave later, looked from one to the other.

"Well, what then, Herr Petersen?" he asked. "I expect Jaenicke will pay the sum out of his legacy?"

"Good heavens, no!" said the engineer, "the legacy isn't by a long way as large as the trustee thought it would be. Herr Jaenicke can't pay the note."

The engineer sat down again. He began to speak of other things than this horrible sheet of stamped paper, and before long he happened to mention that Glauss had once earned a thousand marks by bringing him the plans of the waterworks.

"Herr Petersen!" said Glauss. "You are, I know, a wealthy man. I know something about you; your house is on my beat. You gave me a thousand marks then, as payment for a trifling service, although you no longer needed the plans. Now tell me, need you really be so hard on Ehlers? Can't you think of any way of helping him?"

"Well," said the engineer, "as a matter of fact, I have been trying to think of something. And I have

34

an idea. Now listen, Herr Ehlers, and don't sit there staring blankly into the future!" And then:

"*Donnerwetter!*" cried the engineer, vivaciously. "Man, I see a way to help you! Now listen carefully!"

Ehlers began to feel hopeful, and looked eagerly at his guest.

Petersen explained that he had a friend who was working out the plans of a warship for the German Government. This friend, who was a civil engineer, had two special hobbies: one was hydraulic engineering, and the other was a method of signalling: he had an idea that the system of naval signals might be very greatly simplified. But the poor fellow was only a civil engineer, and he was finding it very difficult to proceed with his studies and his plans, as his inventions were really intended for use in the Navy. Petersen was quite convinced that his friend's ideas were thoroughly practicable, but the trouble was that the inventor had no means of knowing what had already been done, of comparing his inventions with those at present in use. If he could only see the plans of a modern warship for half an hour—for example, the plans of a big cruiser like the *Von der Tann*—and could also have a look at the secret signalling-code of the Navy, he would then be able to judge whether his inventions were likely to be successful.

The marine was visibly startled. Glauss, however, thought highly of the plan, and the engineer said that he would get his friend to come to Wilhelmshaven, and to bring three thousand marks with him, for he was sure that Herr Ehlers would be willing to do him this trifling service.

Now matters moved quickly. Ehlers put up an instinctive and desperate resistance; the note was protested, and the bailiff made his appearance. Glauss kept his friend well in hand; the unfortunate marine was now never quite sober; and one day he appeared with the constructors' plans of the great cruiser, on which he had somehow managed to lay his hands. He went to Glauss's flat, and the two men hurried off to the lonely villa. The engineer took the plans in order to carry them upstairs to show to his brother. Ten minutes later he returned. The plans had told his brother nothing new. Ehlers breathed more freely when the precious sheets were in his hands again; he had been promised that the note should be destroyed when the signal-book had been obtained; and as though the Furies were at his heels he hurried on board with the plans and returned them to their place.

Jaenicke meanwhile had not been idle. Through him Petersen's money found its way into the pockets of yet other officials. Another policeman, Heinrich Suhr, had received some of it, and there were certain other officials who had accepted Jaenicke's hundred-mark notes. In this way the plans of the whole naval port came into Petersen's hands: always for ten minutes only, but that was more than long enough to enable him to photograph the drawings and documents.

At last came the day when Ehlers, trembling with fear, brought Petersen the signal-book, thus betraying one of the most important secrets of the Navy. It was soon returned to him; the official seal was removed from his furniture, the note was torn up, and a few thousand-mark notes were folded away in his pocket-book; but the heart that beat against that pocket-book was now full of apprehension. He had saved his newly-acquired possessions only at the cost of greater fear and anxiety and unrest than had ever been his before. He had just enough intelligence to see that there was a terrible snag somewhere. He did his best to suppress his fears, but in the process he became a hopeless drunkard.

Presently the time came for Glauss to take the remainder of his leave. Once more he travelled in his old waterproof cape to Hamburg; once more, smartly tailored, he boarded the night express to Paris. Once more, for a few days, he became the lover of Yvonne, the girl from Marseilles.

.   .   .   .   .

About this time the German General Staff received a telegram from London which, when deciphered, caused the greatest consternation. The civilian members of the German Intelligence Service were informed of its contents; an agent was sent to London, and when he returned the authorities were paralysed with alarm. The contents of the telegram were confirmed. The German Intelligence Service in London had discovered that the British had had in their hands the signal-book of the German Navy and the plans of the *Von der*

Tann, the swiftest vessel in the battle-fleet, the details of whose construction were a deadly secret.

About the same time one of the most capable criminal commissaries of the Cologne police, an ex-officer of the Army, and now a reserve officer, was sent to Paris on the trail of an international jewel-thief. One morning, as the commissary was leaving his sleeping-car on his way to the restaurant-car, he saw, in the corridor, a rather thickset man, standing with his hands in his pockets and whistling complacently out of the window. The commissary remembered that he had seen this man in the same train a few months earlier. He was puzzled by the traveller's appearance; he was extraordinarily well-dressed, and it did not seem natural that he should be. His coarse hands did not match his fine silk shirt; his behaviour at table was not that of a man used to the refinements of life; in short, the commissary felt so interested that when the passengers' passports were examined he managed to stand immediately behind him. Reading the man's passport over his shoulder, the commissary discovered that this fashionably attired person was a policeman. This was a singular thing; for policemen do not as a rule travel to Paris by first class. The commissary quietly showed his papers to a French police officer at the customs barrier, and managed, unknown to the suspect, to examine his passport more closely. He had made no mistake: the man was a policeman; his name was Glauss, and he came from Wilhelmshaven. At the request of the German commissary his French colleague, who probably thought that the man must be

38

a common criminal, and that the commissary was pursuing him, played a little comedy. He pretended to find that the photograph on the passport did not resemble the traveller. Glauss produced other papers. There was no longer any room for doubt: the first-class passenger was a policeman from Wilhelmshaven.

The commissary decided to ask his superiors to write to the Wilhelmshaven police, in order that they might explain this singular proceeding. He finished his business in Paris, and on the evening before he returned to Germany he went out with a Parisian colleague in search of a night's amusement. They entered one of the smaller and more fashionable dance-halls, and there the commissary suddenly saw before him the mysterious policeman. The man was standing in the cloak-room, taking a long and tender farewell of a pretty, black-haired young woman. He was promising her that he would soon return. He then left the premises while the girl returned to the dancing-floor.

The commissary begged his French colleague to do him a favour. He wanted to have a talk with this pretty little black-haired damsel; he wanted to get something out of her. The French detective readily agreed; the three sat down together, and presently Yvonne, without any pressing, was telling them about the German who had just bidden her good-bye. He must, she said, be very rich; this was the second time he had come to Paris, and each time he had simply thrown his money about. The first time he had received a telegram during the afternoon, while he was in his hotel, and with this telegram in his hand he had immediately visited all the dance-halls to look for her, in order to spend a last night with her.

"I stuck it behind my looking-glass," she said. "It is still there."

When the girl had left the table for a moment the German said to his French colleague:

"I should very much like to see that telegram."

When Yvonne returned the French detective produced his card. The girl was at first greatly alarmed, but she soon recovered her equanimity on learning that all that was required of her was that she should produce the telegram in question.

Next morning the commissary travelled back to Cologne. The telegram which Yvonne had given him did not tell him much. It was addressed to Glauss in Paris; the text consisted of three words: "Return immediately Petersen." It had been given in at Wilhelmshaven.

When the commissary reported to his superiors and informed them of the result of his journey to Paris he did not forget to mention the incident of the policeman who travelled first class.

To his surprise, the chief of the Cologne police betrayed an extraordinary interest in the case; so the commissary produced the telegram which he had taken from behind Yvonne's looking-glass. When his chief had glanced at its contents he gazed at the commissary in bewilderment.

"Man," he said, "do you know what you have proved by this? This is a stupendous affair!"

The commissary looked at him in amazement. His chief pushed a document across the table; the commissary unfolded and read it, and now it was his turn to be astonished. In the document the General Staff requested all the chiefs of police in the country to keep a special watch for foreign secret agents. It stated that it had been established that spies had recently discovered important naval secrets, especially in Wilhelmshaven. The German agents in England had reported, and the fact had been confirmed, that one of the chief spies who had been instructed to ferret out naval secrets was a man of the name of Petersen.

The Cologne authorities immediately sent the commissary, with the impounded telegram, to Berlin. When he returned to Cologne he had in his pocket an order which instructed the Cologne police to make further inquiries in Wilhelmshaven, and to be sparing of neither men nor money. It appeared that the chief spy, Petersen, was stationed in Wilhelmshaven, and that the policeman, Glauss, must have played some part in the betrayal of naval secrets.

Now events followed fast on one another. Glauss was kept under observation; and it was noted that he was constantly in the company of Jaenicke, Suhr and Ehlers. The police soon ascertained that all four had more money than they could have come by honestly, and that Ehlers had furnished a flat at a cost of several thousands of marks. Watching them day and night, the detectives noted that every morning Glauss and Jaenicke paid a visit to the lonely villa. And now the Cologne police, who had said nothing of their proceedings to the Wilhelmshaven authorities, as they wished the fact that they were on the track of the spies to remain a secret, resolved on a decisive stroke. Very early one morning the policemen, Jaenicke and Glauss, were arrested in their homes and confined in separate cells. Ehlers was arrested on board the *Von der Tann*.

The commissary in charge of operations had a fair knowledge of human nature. He left the two policemen to meditate quietly in their cells, and confined his attention to Ehlers. After an hour's interrogation Ehlers' resistance was at an end. He confessed that he had, at the instance of Glauss, shown the plans of the cruiser, and the signal-book, to the engineer, Petersen, and having confessed so much he broke down altogether. He told the sympathetic-looking commissary all the ins and outs of the affair, and what he knew of the doings of Glauss and Jaenicke. He did not forget to tell the policeman that Glauss had obtained the plans of the waterworks for Petersen, and Jaenicke the plans of the port. In conclusion, he confessed that he had been afraid all along that he had fallen into the hands of spies, and now that it was too late he bitterly regretted that he had not reported the whole affair to his commander after his first interview with Petersen.

The commissary now set a ring of watchers round the villa. He could not make any immediate arrests, for it seemed that the house had been empty for some days. He sent a detective, disguised as an employé of the gas company, to the house; the door was opened by a woman servant; and as far as the detective could tell there was nothing particularly suspicious about the house.

Meanwhile the detectives had been looking for the policeman, Suhr, but were unable to arrest him; he had apparently heard of the arrest of Glauss and Jaenicke, and had immediately decamped. There was now, of course, a danger that it would be impossible to apprehend Petersen and his accomplices, for Suhr would probably have warned them. There was no means of knowing how many more persons in official positions were involved in the affair; but it was ascertained later that Glauss and Jaenicke, acting for Petersen, had enlisted an alarming number of policemen and other persons as spies.

For a few days longer the detectives, keeping under cover, continued to watch the villa. And one night a motor-car suddenly came rushing down the silent street. The car stopped; the headlights were immediately switched off, and the occupants—three men and a woman—walked quickly through the garden and disappeared into the house. The commissary now brought his men into the open. Twenty strong, revolver in hand, they drew a cordon round the house, and presently the commissary knocked at the door. No one answered his knock. A glimmer of light could be seen through the carefully-drawn curtains. The commissary tugged at the bell and hammered at the door, but no one opened. He then, without more ado, broke one of the ground-floor windows, and entered the house with two of his men. A few more followed, and proceeded to search the house. To their amazement, it was empty. All the doors stood open, with the exception of one on the first floor. It did not long resist the fists and shoulders of the policemen. When they had burst it in they found a room equipped like a photographer's studio. There were maps everywhere; there were large copying-cameras; and powerful electric lights hung from the ceiling. In one corner lay a bundle of photographs, and among them was one of Glauss and Jaenicke breaking into the counting-house of a brewery.

The commissary turned the whole house upside down; he sent some of his men to search the loft, and he himself, accompanied by others, went down into the cellar. Here too the search was at first fruitless; but then the wine-cellar was found, and it was noticed that a bottle-rack had been moved away from the wall. In the wall was an aperture, the height of a man.

The detectives switched on their flash-lamps, climbed into the opening, and found themselves in an underground passage which ran straight ahead, and after following it for several hundred yards they found themselves in another cellar. On going upstairs they discovered that they were in a villa which stood not far from Petersen's house, and had been unoccupied for years.

This explained how it was that the inhabitants of the smaller villa, and among them Petersen himself, had dared to re-enter their house, although it was surrounded by watchers. Apparently they were not in Wilhelmshaven when the two policemen were arrested, but, being warned of the arrests by an accomplice, they had returned in order to remove such important papers as were left in the house. This they had succeeded in doing. The woman who had been taken for a servant had fled with them.

The motor-car which was standing before the house was of course impounded, but it had to be surrendered, as it belonged to a garage proprietor in Hamburg, who had no connection with the fugitives.

Late that night, and in a very depressed mood, the commissary returned to his hotel. In the hall sat a detective whom he had brought from Cologne, and who had not taken part in the raid. This man had been posted in the prison, in order to keep an eye on the prisoners. When he saw the commissary enter he sprang up and announced that Glauss had escaped from custody about two hours earlier. The commissary turned pale. He drove immediately to the prison, where he learned that Glauss had apparently made his escape with the help of several confederates.

When the overseer, after inspecting his cell that night, had closed the door, Glauss had thrust the bristles of a brush between the door and the hasp of the lock, so that the bolt had not shot home. During the night he had opened the door, run along the corridor, opened an upstairs window, and clambered on to the roof. He had descended to earth by means of the fire-escape, and

his further flight was to be explained only by the supposition that someone outside the prison wall had
thrown him a rope ladder. That same night it was
stated by various witnesses that a motor-car had been
seen waiting in the neighbourhood of the prison, and the
personal description of the man who was standing beside the car fitted to a hair the English spy who had
passed in Germany as the engineer Petersen.

For a long while nothing was heard of Glauss, but
the German agents in England were on the look-out,
and one day they sent word to Berlin that Glauss had
arrived in London from Paris, and was living in a
cheap boarding-house.

The Cologne commissary went to London, bearing
a letter from the German Government, which requested
the British authorities to arrest the runaway policeman
and hand him over for trial. The British authorities
at first refused to do so, since it was not in accordance
with international law to permit extradition for espionage. The commissary smiled politely, and explained
that there was no question of espionage; but that Glauss
was suspected of having committed a number of burglaries in Germany. The evidence against him was
convincing. . . . In the end, Glauss was handed over.

The final act of this affair was played out in several
scenes. On the 26th June, 1913, the High Court of
Justice found Jaenicke guilty of espionage, and sentenced him to six years' imprisonment; this, with a
term of three years' imprisonment which had already
been inflicted on him for burglary, meant a total of

nine years' imprisonment. The prisoner was a sergeant in the Landwehr; he was married, and the father of two children. Ehlers was sentenced on the 27th June, 1912. The presiding judge on this occasion was Dr. Menge, the President of the Senate, a white-bearded, patriarchal figure. Both Ehlers and Jaenicke were tried secretly, the public being refused admission to the court. Ehlers, who confessed to his guilt, was sentenced to six years' imprisonment and discharged from the Service.

Glauss was tried on the 9th March, 1912. Since he could not be accused of espionage, he was charged at the Aurich assizes with seven acts of burglary. He was sentenced to six years' imprisonment.

In December, 1911, something occurred which revealed the magnitude and the purposeful nature of the English secret service organization in Germany. Lieutenant Steinbrink, of the North Sea fleet, was sent from Wilhelmshaven to Kiel with the whole of the secret documents relating to the Petersen affair. In the Hamburg terminus the wallet in which he was carrying these inexpressibly important papers was stolen from him, and so dexterously that it was some time before he discovered his loss. As far as the lieutenant was concerned there was an unpleasant sequel to the affair. The Berlin *Morgenpost* for the 4th February, 1912, contained the following announcement:

"It is announced by telegram that the Wilhelmshaven court martial has found First-Lieutenant Stein-

47

brink guilty of disobedience which resulted in the loss of secret documents, and has sentenced him to one year's detention in a fortress."

At the conclusion of this affair, which caused a tremendous sensation in the years immediately preceding the war, there was a brisk campaign of public opinion against the negligence on the part of the authorities which had made such a case of espionage possible.

The full extent of the affair—of which the particular case which we have described was only a part—may be judged from another announcement in the Berlin *Morgenpost* of the 11th February:

"Information has reached us from Essen, in the Ruhr, to the effect that the entire police force of Wilhelmshaven is to be transferred, from the highest official to the lowest. The police authorities in the industrial area have been requested to submit the names of policemen who are willing to be transferred to Wilhelmshaven."

CHAPTER THREE

COLONEL REDL OF THE AUSTRIAN IMPERIAL STAFF

THE Prague correspondent of the Berlin newspaper *B.Z. am Mittag*, who was also the editor of the Prague newspaper *Bohemia*, reported to his Berlin editor, on the 26th May, 1913, that the Chief of the General Staff of the Prague Division of the Austrian Army, Colonel Alfred Redl, had shot himself in a Vienna hotel.

On the 27th May he telephoned to his Berlin editor:

THE CHIEF OF THE GENERAL STAFF A SPY?

(*From our own Correspondent*)

"*Prague, 27th May*, 1913: Sensational rumours are in circulation here respecting the suicide of the Chief of the General Staff of the Prague (9th) Army Corps, Colonel Redl, who on Sunday killed himself in a Vienna hotel. These rumours are to the effect that the officer's suicide was not unconnected with a recently discovered case of espionage. Colonel Redl came of a family in poor circumstances, but lived in an extravagant style. It is said that he had been ordered to report at the War Office on the day following the date of his suicide. Colonel Redl was the official prosecutor for the Ministry of War in cases of espionage, and in this way came into contact with circles which would afford him an opportunity of abusing his position."

This notice appeared first of all in the Berlin *B.Z. am Mittag*. Although the editor of the Prague *Bohemia* knew perfectly well that the Colonel had been strongly suspected of espionage, and although he could guess the reason of his suicide, he thought it better that the news should be published first in a Berlin paper. In that case it would not be possible for the Austrian censorship to hush the matter up, and he felt as a good Austrian that it was highly undesirable that the truth should be suppressed. If the news had made its first appearance in the Prague *Bohemia* it would, in all probability, never have reached the public, as the paper would at once have been censored, and possibly suppressed and even sequestrated, which, apart from everything else, would have meant a serious loss to the publisher. The *B.Z. am Mittag* was beyond the reach of the Austrian censor; and the editor had not miscalculated, for shortly after the appearance of the paper there was a great commotion in Austrian military circles. The same afternoon the German General Staff asked the military authorities in Vienna for the facts of the case. The correspondents of all the leading newspapers of the world besieged the Ministry of War in Vienna in their eagerness to obtain further details; while the officers of the Austrian General Staff besieged the coroner's office, in order that they might learn the truth of the matter. The Kaiser Franz

Joseph had been informed of the affair by noon, and that night the special correspondents of the great international news agencies foregathered in Prague and Vienna. These were men of wide experience, and experts in their calling, and although the Austrian authorities had given the most stringent orders that no information was to be divulged, it was not long before the correspondents had elicited the main features of the affair, and the public learned, to its amazement, that Colonel Redl, an officer of the Austrian General Staff, who had long been the official prosecutor for the War Office in cases of espionage, had for years been in the pay of the Russian secret service, and had sold to Russia everything worth knowing about the Austrian Army, and also, in all probability, such German secrets as were accessible to him.

While the newspapers of every country but Austria had published this news, with "scare" headings, on their front pages, the Austrian journals, thanks to the extraordinarily strict censorship, had not as yet succeeded in informing their readers of the tragedy. But the ingenious editor of *Bohemia* was not to be beaten. In his evening edition he published, where it would catch the reader's eye, a *denial* of the statements which had appeared in the foreign Press.

"We have been requested by a high authority to contradict the rumours which have been circulating, especially in military circles, to the effect that the Chief of the General Staff of the Prague Army Corps,

Colonel Alfred Redl, who, as our readers are aware, committed suicide the day before yesterday in Vienna, had been guilty of betraying military secrets and that he was a spy in Russian pay. The commission which has been dispatched to Prague, consisting of a colonel and a major, who on Sunday, in the presence of the commanding officer of the Prague Army Corps, Baron Giesl, proceeded to the late officer's quarters and examined his papers, was instructed to inquire into delinquencies of quite another character."

As the editor had calculated, the issue in which this paragraph appeared was not suppressed, since the censors had no means of knowing who the "high authority" might be, and had no suspicion that this "authority" had no existence.

Now the scandal was the property of the public, and the details which transpired showed that this was the most wholesale case of espionage ever known in Europe. Alfred Redl came of a poor and obscure family, and was no more than a boy when he entered the Austrian Army. Being of middle-class origin, and having no social influence which might hasten his promotion, he applied himself assiduously to the study of military science. Intensely ambitious as he was, he soon attracted the attention of his superiors, and was given his majority, and appointed to the head of the Intelligence Service of the Austrian Army. There were indications that soon after his appointment he had begun to work for Russia. In his position he had to give special attention to the work of counter-espionage, and as an expert member of the court before which those accused of espionage were tried he had not displayed excessive severity; indeed, the prisoners whom he prosecuted were almost always acquitted. It was natural that Redl, to whom fell the task of organizing the active espionage undertaken by Austria—principally against Russia—and also the counter-espionage, should come into contact with all sorts and conditions of spies. It was, of course, known in Russia that Redl was particularly skilful in detecting Russian spies. It was incumbent on the Russian Intelligence Service to draw the claws of this dangerous fellow, if that was anyhow possible. Among the many persons who had dealings with Redl as chief of the Austrian Intelligence Service there were some who were in the pay of Russia, and who, during their brief sojourns in Austria, could find all sorts of pretexts for obtaining access to Redl. In accordance with the time-honoured method, many dazzlingly beautiful women of every type and race began to cross this dangerous officer's path, but strangely enough they never succeeded in attracting his attention.

The name of the Russian agent who contrived to secure the services of Major Redl for his country is unknown to history. This agent, whoever he may have been, discovered that the officer had a certain weakness, which, if he wished to remain in the Army, he must never allow to appear. He was quite insensitive to the charms of women; he was a man of homosexual tendencies. The Austrian staff officer was the victim of a truly diabolical scheme. Now not women but men began to cross his path, and these men obtained a hold over him. This went on for months, and then one day the Russian agent called at Major Redl's office. In the *Neuen Berliner Zeitung* of 25th February, 1924, the following description appeared of Major Redl's office, from the pen of Egon Kisch, a journalist who knew the ins and outs of the "Redl affair."

"All secret callers were photographed full face and in profile, without their knowledge. In two pictures which were hanging on the wall were apertures for the lenses of cameras which were operated from the adjacent room. Similarly, every caller could be made, without his knowledge, to leave his finger-prints. The officer, reaching for the telephone, would hand his visitor a cigar-case (or a bonbonnière in the case of a woman) which had received an imperceptible coating of minium, and the match-box and ash-tray which the smoker had to handle were similarly prepared. If the visitor declined both cigar-case and bonbonnière, Major Redl was called out of the room. If the caller was a spy by profession he was certain to pick up the document which lay ready on the table, marked 'Strictly secret.' This document was prepared with a special powder. In a small cupboard on the wall, which had the appearance of a medicine-chest, a sound-box and listening-tube were installed, for the benefit of the shorthand-writer in the next room, but if desired the conversation could be recorded on a gramophone disc."

All this elaborate equipment was of no avail against the Russian agent who now entered the room. After his first few words the Major shut off the listening-tube, and by the close of an interview which lasted for some hours the loyal Austrian officer had become a Russian spy. He had taken the money which his visitor offered him; and at the same time the Russian had handed him a bundle of documents in which his moral delinquencies of the past few months were described with painful exactitude. Some may ask why the Austrian officer did not arrest the blackmailer—who must have admitted that he was a Russian spy—and leave the service, adopting some other profession? The answer, presumably, is that he was tender of his reputation; that he feared public opinion.

From this time onwards Redl, in return for very large sums of money, gave the Russian Intelligence Service all that it wished to know. He photographed the plans of all the Austrian fortresses and frontier defences, and all documents of importance, and gave the photographs to the enemy.

In the year 1903 his Russian taskmasters requested him to furnish the mobilization plans of the Austro-Hungarian Army, which had been drawn up by the Austrian General Staff in view of the possibility of an Austro-Russian war. Redl did not hesitate to photograph even this most secret of documents, thereby striking a blow against his own army, which, together with other exploits of his, did it such grievous injury that even by the outbreak of the war of 1914 the harm had not been fully repaired.

With the delivery of the plans of mobilization Redl entered upon a kind of activity which was even more disastrous to the Austrian Army. To begin with, something quite unexpected happened. For some considerable time, even before Redl had received his appointment, the Austrian Intelligence Service had employed a Russian officer on the Warsaw Staff, whose information was exceptionally accurate, and who did his work with great adroitness. This Russian was the chief instrument of the Austrian counter-espionage against Russia. One day he informed Vienna that the Russians had in their possession the Austrian plans of mobilization, with all details. This was a most startling piece of news, and all the officers of the Austrian General Staff—with the exception, of course, of Major Redl, who had himself sold the plans—were profoundly shocked and amazed. As a matter of course the task of discovering the man who had sold the plans fell to Major Redl, the chief of the counter-espionage bureau. The affair had excited such intense feeling that Redl, if he wished to retain his position, was really obliged to discover and arrest the traitor. He proceeded to make all sorts of investigations, and one day he suddenly disappeared. No one knew where he had gone; no one knows to-day; but wherever he went, he suddenly reappeared in his office, and informed the authorities that he had ascertained, almost beyond a doubt, that the guilty persons were Chief Auditor Hekailo of the Lemberg Command, Major Ritter von Wienkowsky of the District Command in Stanislau, and the personal adjutant of the military commandant of Lemberg, Captain Acht. The auditor Hekailo fled while the strictly secret inquiry was in progress, and it then appeared that he had forged a receipt in order to conceal the embezzlement of military funds.

Hekailo was arrested in Brazil. He produced a Russian passport, placed himself under the protection of the Russian Consulate, and asserted that he was a Russian subject. He had never heard of a Herr Hekailo. But the Brazilian police found in his trunk an Austrian military tunic, which he had packed by inadvertence in the excitement of his headlong flight. He was extradited on the charge of embezzlement, and confessed in Vienna, that he had acted as a Russian spy. Since the laws of international extradition made it impossible to try him in Austria for espionage, he confessed to his misdeeds quite openly, but denied the most essential charge—that he had supplied the Russians with the plans of mobilization.

The officers Acht and Wienkowsky were likewise arrested, and they too confessed to acts of espionage, but only when Redl confronted them with letters which they had written to officers of the Russian Intelligence Service. Whence these letters were obtained was Redl's secret. But he claimed to have "paid to a person unknown for furnishing evidence, twenty thousand kronen."

In order to fill a small gap in the evidence against the three prisoners, Redl proposed that the commission of inquiry should request the Russian staff officer in Warsaw, who was in the Austrian Service, to send certain secret documents of the central bureau to Vienna. The requisite instructions were sent, and as the Russian was attempting to carry them out—as he was in the act of removing a certain bundle of documents from the files in one of the rooms of the headquarters of the General Staff in Warsaw, which he had entered by means of a skeleton key—the door of the room opened, and three Russian officers confronted him, covering him with their revolvers, and arrested him.

We know to-day that Redl had persuaded his Russian friends to surrender Hekailo, Acht and Wienkowsky in order to bring off a successful *coup*. They even provided him with evidence against them. But they demanded a certain service in return. He must deliver up to them the most dangerous Austrian spy in Russia—who was, as a matter of fact, the Russian staff officer in Warsaw. Redl, as agreed, lured him into a trap, and after a hurried trial the man was hanged. Hekailo, Acht and Wienkowsky, despite their denials, were found by the commission of inquiry to be guilty of stealing the plans of mobilization; a not unreasonable assumption, since it was proved that they had acted as spies in the pay of Russia. And then it seemed as though the proceedings against the three officers would take a different turn. Redl, during the course of the trial, suddenly declared that he was now convinced that Hekailo alone had sold the plans, and that Acht and Wienkowsky were innocent. This assertion of Redl's, who had himself furnished the evidence incriminating the two officers, was of no avail, and they were both sentenced to long terms of imprisonment. Redl had been ordered by his Russian paymasters to save the two men, as they could still serve their country as active officers; but he was unable to do so. Angered by his failure, the Russians made even more exacting demands of him. It was no longer enough that he should betray the secrets of the Austrian Army; he was ordered to furnish the names of all the Austrian spies at work in Russia. The Austrian secret service now suffered blow after blow. Some of the most efficient Austrian spies in Russia were suddenly arrested; while others, newly enlisted and freshly trained, were no sooner sent across the frontier than they suffered the same dreadful fate; and no one could explain how these things were possible. In the year 1912 something occurred which was the culmination of all that had preceded it, and which caused the greatest alarm, even in Court circles, by reason of its mysterious circumstances; for at that time no one was able to solve the riddle.

The heir to the throne, Franz Ferdinand, had paid a country visit to the Tsar, and in his retinue was the Austro-Hungarian Military Attaché, Lieutenant-Colonel Müller. In Warsaw, as the Austrians were on their way home, a Russian colonel, an officer of the General

Staff, introduced himself to Müller, and offered him the secret plans of mobilization against Austria, for which he asked a very great price. Müller dealt with the matter without consulting the Intelligence Bureau in Vienna. He induced the Austrian General Staff to send an officer, in mufti, provided with a false passport, and the sum demanded, to Warsaw. The plans were delivered and paid for. The Russian colonel, however, was immediately betrayed, by Redl, to his own countrymen. He shot himself as he was about to be arrested.

But the most valuable service which Redl ever rendered to the Russians was of a different nature. He systematically suppressed such reports of the Austrian agents in Russia as announced an increase in the strength of the Russian Army. If a spy was so efficient as to report such increases on several successive occasions, Redl betrayed the man to the Russians. The result was that on the outbreak of the Great War the Russians possessed seventy-four more divisions of active troops than was suspected in Austria—or in Germany either.

The exposure of Redl came about in a singular fashion. Like all officers of the General Staff, he was instructed to proceed to the front for a time, in order that he should not lose touch with the active troops. He was appointed Chief of Staff to a Prague division, and it was generally understood that after serving with this division the ambitious officer would be promoted on his return to the General Staff. During his service in Prague his successor at the head of the Intelligence

Service secretly instituted a so-called "black cabinet," disregarding the law of the country relating to the secrecy of postal correspondence, and opened, day by day, all letters whose senders or recipients aroused suspicion. The attention of the "cabinet" was called to two letters, addressed to "Opernball 13," which were lying in the central post office in Vienna. These letters were opened. One of them contained six thousand kronen; the other eight thousand. These remittances appeared suspicious; above all, because these large sums of money were sent by the ordinary post, instead of being registered or insured, and because both letters were posted at Eydtkuhnen, on the Russian frontier. In order to arrest the recipient of these letters, who had already been suspected of espionage, two detectives were concealed in one of the rooms of the post office. In this room was a bell which could be rung from the counter of the *poste restante*. For weeks the two detectives sat in this room, smoking innumerable cigarettes and playing cards, and feeling terribly bored. And then, one afternoon, the bell rang. The detectives rushed along the corridor. When they entered the post office they were met by the clerk who was on duty at the counter of the *poste restante*. The two letters had just been fetched; the man to whom they were given had already left the post office! The detectives, accompanied by the clerk, ran out into the street, in time to see a man whom the clerk declared to be the recipient of the letters jump into a taxi and drive off. The detectives noted the number of the taxi, and by good fortune it was not long before they found it again. It was then unoccupied. They hailed it, and learned that the man for whom they were looking had gone into a café. They jumped into the cab, in order to drive to the café, and found, between the cushions, the leather sheath of a pocket-knife. Once more they were in luck; they learned that the man whom they were following had driven from the café to the Hôtel Klomser. The porter of the hotel declared at first that he knew nothing of the man who had recently driven up to the hotel. The detectives examined the hotel register, and there found the name of Colonel Redl, who was then staying in the hotel. They considered whether they should not at once go to him and put the case before him, for they knew that no one was more familiar with all the intricacies of foreign espionage. While they were standing in the hotel lobby one of the detectives happened to feel in the pocket of his cloak; his fingers closed on the leather case which he had found in the taxi; and an idea occurred to him. He gave the sheath to the porter, and instructed him to ask each of the guests in the hotel whether he had by any chance lost the thing. He had not finished speaking when suddenly Colonel Redl, the divisional Chief of Staff, appeared in full uniform on the stairs of the hotel. The two detectives assumed a respectful bearing, and the one who had been speaking to the porter tried to hold him back; but the man, faithful to his instructions, suddenly went up to the colonel with the leather sheath in his hand, and asked him:

"Has the Herr Colonel perhaps lost this case recently?"

The colonel felt in his pockets abstractedly, brought out his knife, looked at the sheath, and answered:

"Yes, of course; thanks very much, that is mine!"

So saying, he left the lobby. The two detectives turned pale. They gazed at one another helplessly; then, in a flash, they were in the street, following the officer. But the colonel too turned pale as he strode swiftly down the street, for he had suddenly realized where he must have left the sheath of his pocket-knife. It was in the taxi; he had used his knife to open the two packages. He felt instinctively that the men who had been standing beside the porter when the latter handed him the sheath were policemen, and that by some unimaginable accident he had been detected. He at once altered his direction; he would go to the garage in which his car was kept; he could still escape and save his life. . . . But then his glance fell on a mirror in a watchmaker's window, and he saw that the detectives were following him. Now he knew that he was lost. An icy shudder ran down his spine; he turned aimlessly into a narrow passage, took from his breast-pocket a bundle of letters which would have proved, beyond a doubt, the extent of his crimes, tore them into shreds, and scattered them on the ground. It had suddenly occurred to him that the detectives might stop to pick up these fragments. But the detectives were no fools; one stopped to pick up the scraps of paper, and the other followed the colonel.

For hours Redl wandered through the streets of Vienna, followed by the detective, and he could not see any means of drawing his head out of the noose.

But during these hours his fate had already been decided. When the detectives had left the hotel to follow Redl, one of them had spoken to a policeman in the street, quickly showing him his papers, and had instructed the man to call up a certain number on the telephone—it was the number of the Secret State Police —and to inform the official who answered his call that "it was all in order, the letters had been fetched by Colonel Redl." When this message was received at the office of the State Police the officer in charge clapped his hands to his head and asked himself whether the two detectives had not suddenly lost their senses. Nevertheless, he dispatched an officer to fetch the receipt given for the letters from the post office, and took immediate steps to obtain some documents in Redl's handwriting from the Ministry of War; and he turned pale when he was forced to admit to himself that the receipt was undoubtedly signed by Redl. He still believed that the matter might have some innocent explanation; it was still possible that Redl had some special and secret task in hand which involved the receipt of these sums of money. But then, breathless and excited, a detective rushed into the room, and spread out before him the torn scraps of paper which Colonel Redl had thrown away while he was being followed. They were fitted together; and it was seen

64

that the torn papers were receipts for letters sent to foreign addresses, and that these addresses were one and all the addresses of foreign intelligence bureaux! And besides the receipts there were some letters which proved beyond a doubt that Colonel Redl was a spy.

The chief of the intelligence bureau of the Austrian General Staff, Colonel von Urbanski, Colonel Redl's successor, sat long in his office, unable to grasp the facts which had been discovered.

Colonel Redl in the meanwhile had pulled himself together. He saw that he could not escape from the detective, who was following him implacably, and went back to his hotel, where an old friend with whom he had intended to spend the evening was awaiting him. This was a high official of the Supreme Court of Justice of Vienna, the Attorney-General, Dr. Victor Pollack, an intimate friend of the colonel's. Redl and Pollack went into the hotel dining-room, and suddenly the colonel came out with the truth. He pushed the plates and glasses aside, leaned heavily on the table, and began to speak. He spoke confusedly and incoherently, telling his friend, the Attorney-General, that he had been guilty of moral delinquencies; he accused himself of a serious crime; he spoke on and on, so that the lawyer could only listen in shocked amazement. He did not say in so many words what it was that he had done; the word "espionage" was not mentioned; he only hinted that he was already pursued by the police, and implored his friend to call up the political police and obtain permission for him to return that same night to his house in Prague, where he would hold himself at the disposal of his superiors. It is possible that he still had thoughts of escaping across the frontier.

The Attorney-General hardly knew what to make of his friend's confusion, but he went to the telephone and called up the political police, and a high official told him that Colonel Redl need not excite himself; he had better go quietly to bed in his hotel. It was impossible to discuss the matter that night. The Attorney-General gathered from the conversation that something really was known against his friend. When he returned to the dining-room Redl sat staring at the wall without a word. When he heard that he was advised to remain in the hotel he got up and went to his room. Greatly disturbed, the Attorney-General took leave of his friend.

Meanwhile the chief of the intelligence bureau of the General Staff, Colonel von Urbanski, had collected his thoughts. He went to the telephone, and learned that the Chief of the General Staff of the Austrian Army, Conrad von Hötzendorff, was at supper in the Grand Hotel. Colonel von Urbanski went thither, led the General out of the dining-room into one of the conference-rooms, told him briefly what had occurred, and proved to him, by means of the torn documents, which had now been carefully fitted together, that a high officer of the Austrian Army, who had filled a position of a specially confidential nature—namely, Colonel

Redl—was a Russian spy. Conrad von Hötzendorff pressed his hands to his heart; then he controlled himself, and gave orders that the affair must be settled and done with that same night; that very night Colonel Redl must die, and the public must not be allowed to obtain the slightest knowledge of this terrible affair. On the following day officers must proceed to Prague and seize all papers and documents to be found in Redl's quarters.

That night Colonel von Urbanski fetched a few of his comrades from their beds, and about midnight four officers knocked at the door of Colonel Redl's room in the Hôtel Klomser. When they entered Redl was standing, in civilian clothes, beside the writing-table, on which lay letters of farewell. As Colonel von Urbanski began to speak, Redl made a weary gesture with his hand, and interrupted him:

"I know why you gentlemen are here. I beg you to ask no questions. I have had no accomplices, and all details will be learned from the papers in my house, which, I suppose, have already been seized."

He was silent; and suddenly one of the officers asked him:

"Have you a revolver by you, *Herr* Redl?"

"No," said Redl.

The officer who had asked the question turned sharply round, hurried to his house, loaded a revolver, and returned with it to the hotel, where his three comrades were sitting in the lobby, waiting. He went up to Redl's room, laid the revolver on the desk, and left the room without a word.

An hour after midnight the bullet was fired that made an end of Colonel Redl's troubles, but the four officers, who had not heard the shot, waited until the dawn in the street before the hotel, to make certain that Redl did not escape.

A wave of indignation passed over Austria when it was learned that a high officer of the Austrian Army was a Russian spy. Everywhere this extraordinary case of espionage was the subject of excited discussion. Nevertheless, the military authorities refused to admit that an officer of the General Staff, filling such a high appointment, had been guilty of spying for a foreign power. The Vienna command made all preparations for the burial of Colonel of the Royal and Imperial Staff Alfred Redl with full military honours. Three battalions of infantry were to lead the funeral procession, and the wreaths and flowers for the stately funeral were already ordered. But by the morning of the day on which Redl was to be laid in his grave the scandal had assumed such dimensions that it was simply impossible to conceal the truth. The following order was dispatched to the commanding officer of the troops which were to have attended the funeral:

"The burial of the late Herr Alfred Redl, formerly Colonel, will be effected as quietly as possible. The directions contained in the orders of the Fortress Commandant of yesterday's date are herewith cancelled."

At midday a plain hearse, unaccompanied, set off at a trot and proceeded to the Central Cemetery, where Grave No. 38, Row 29, Group 79, received the body of Alfred Redl.

CHAPTER FOUR

AN IDEAL SPY

IN July, 1912, the German spy Armgard Karl Graves was tried in Edinburgh. In the course of the proceedings the precise nature and extent of Graves's exploits was revealed; and to each item of incriminating evidence the accused replied with a polite and amiable nod. Suddenly the judge exclaimed: "But you are really an ideal spy!"

To relate the history of this ideal spy is to describe a battle between two masters in the art of espionage. One of the protagonists was the German spy Graves; the other the British officer and spy, Captain Trench, whose name has been mentioned elsewhere in this book.

Captain Trench was one of the principal agents of the British Intelligence Service, and both before and during the war was always to the front where a critical piece of espionage had to be undertaken.

Armgard Karl Graves entered the German Intelligence Service some years before the war. He had studied mathematics and engineering in the technical schools of his country, and he was enlisted in the service because of his expert knowledge of armaments. In 1910 he crossed the North Sea. He had been set a definite task: he was to discover what guns the firm of

Beardmore & Co. in Glasgow were manufacturing. The Beardmore works were engaged in the manufacture of certain guns for the British Navy which were of unusually large calibre, and were equipped with a new type of mounting, and novel traversing and elevating mechanisms, to say nothing of sights and periscopes, and all sorts of technical refinements which were as yet unknown in Germany. Above all, the Germans were convinced that the range-finders which the firm was manufacturing were better than their own appliances; so this matter too must be investigated, lest the Fatherland should be left in the rear.

To begin with, Karl Graves transformed himself into a Swiss citizen. He procured the necessary papers, and before proceeding to Scotland he spent some time in a watchmaking factory, so that he could represent himself to be a journeyman watchmaker. Such a trifle as forging references from a Swiss factory whose watches and clocks are known all the world over presented no serious difficulty to an intelligence bureau. Thus equipped, Graves went first of all to London. He went no farther for a time, as he wished to look about him and complete his knowledge of the English language, and also to learn something of the shipping lines, and generally to take his bearings. Then he went north to Glasgow. There he took a room in a cheap and modest boarding-house, and proceeded at his leisure to look for work.

First of all he thoroughly explored the city. He was in no hurry to get work; as he told his landlady, he had a little money put by; he had been paid good wages in Switzerland. Finally, after a few weeks, he found work with a cabinet-maker who had a large workshop, and did a good business in grandfather clocks. This business had developed to such an extent that the proprietor urgently needed a skilled man to regulate the clocks after they had been fitted into their cases, to do such repairs as were necessary, and in short to undertake all such work as was connected with the actual clocks. Graves haggled for some time over the wages which he was to receive, but finally an agreement was reached. For some weeks the new employé seemed to take no interest in anything beyond his work. He was, however, an easy man to get on with, as he soon made a particular friend of a turner who was employed in the workshop. This turner was full of troubles; he told the clockmaker that he had a large family to feed, and that his wages were quite insufficient to supply all their wants. Still, one of his boys was already earning good money; and it was easy to see that he was very proud of this boy. He was the eldest son, and had been sent to a good school. He had a talent for drawing, and had obtained a post in the drawing-office of the Beard-more works, where he had to make working drawings of details for use in the various departments.

Of this son, who was an educated man, "and wore a clean collar even on weekdays," the father had a high opinion; and as the friendship between the clockmaker and the turner grew more and more intimate, there came a day when the two of them went to meet the young man as he left the drawing-office. They waited outside the great gates of the works until the crowd of workers came out, when they met the young draughtsman and went home together. Some time later the clockmaker complained that he was not comfortable in his boarding-house; the landlady was an old vixen, who put every jug of hot water on the bill as an "extra," and there was no one there with whom he could talk of an evening. He spoke so often of his intention of seeking other quarters that the turner finally told his wife that his friend the clockmaker was looking for a furnished room. On the following day the turner casually mentioned that if the clockmaker still thought of moving he might perhaps consider the possibility of coming to them. There was still a room to spare in the house; it was small, certainly, but the bed was comfortable, and what was more important, he could have it cheap. If he liked he could have his meals with them too; they had only to come to an arrangement about the price.

Needless to say, the men agreed about the price, and the clockmaker went to live with the turner, and so it came about, quite naturally, that he spent the evenings with the young draughtsman, telling him of his travels, and his work, and of the many great factories which he had seen in Europe.

The draughtsman took great pleasure in his company —he was such a good talker. He in his turn told his new friend about the works in whose drawing-office he was employed, while the clockmaker described the method of preparing working drawings in other branches of engineering. The draughtsman, too, had something to say on the subject; in short, they spent hours together talking shop.

One day the son came home with a great piece of news. Beardmore's had received such important Government contracts for the construction of naval guns that they were obliged to work overtime. Day and night shifts had been organized in every department of the works, and even the drawing-office was working overtime, as they now had to copy and enlarge the drawings of the epicyclic gear, which was difficult work, demanding the greatest accuracy. It was about this time that the clockmaker began to feel discontented with his work at the cabinet-maker's; and one day he declared that he would see, some time or other, whether he couldn't get work at Beardmore's, in the department where the gearing was assembled. He asked where the offices were, and he himself went thither to make inquiries, but nothing came of his application, as no foreign subjects were employed on work of this kind.

Greatly dejected, he left the office of the works; but on the way out—which took him all over the works— he asked to be directed to the drawing-office in which his friend was working. He looked in, spoke a word or two to his friend, and hurried home.

Hitherto Graves had lived the life of an industrious and reliable workman. Now he began to display quite other qualities.

He knew, from the draughtsman's conversation, how the hours were arranged in the drawing-office. The room in which his friend was working, and which Graves had already noted on his visit to the works, was on the ground floor of a long, one-storied building. The room was a small one. Two men were constantly at work there, before a wide, low window, and at night a great arc-lamp shone outside this window: one of many which turned the night to day in the Beardmore yards. During the week when Graves thought of beginning operations the draughtsman was on the night shift. At eight o'clock in the evening he relieved one of the two draughtsmen who were on the day shift, and the night shift left the office at four o'clock in the morning. From four to eight in the morning no one was working in the room. The charwomen appeared about seven o'clock.

In this office the working drawings of the epicyclic gear were copied. The originals were kept in an iron safe let into the wall, which was opened with two keys. One pair of keys was retained by Graves's friend; the other pair (there being four keys in all) by one of the other draughtsmen.

In his leisure hours Karl Graves practised a hobby. He was an amateur photographer, and something of an artist also; and his friend often served him as a model. He drew the draughtsman's face full-face, three-quarter-face, and in profile; he painted his portrait in water-colours, and he photographed him.

One winter morning, about half-past five, the draughtsman came home from his work on the night shift. When he had been in bed for perhaps a quarter of an hour Karl Graves cautiously lit a candle in his room and went to the looking-glass. He was of the same build as the draughtsman: slender and sinewy. But his hair was thick and black; while the draughtsman's was red and bristly. But now a red wig was drawn over his black hair, and the face of Herr Graves was unrecognizable. It was much younger; the lines round the mouth were different; the mouth itself was altered, and the nose was the nose of the draughtsman.

Graves threw the light on his face as he stood before the mirror. He drew the wig a little farther over his forehead, gave a last touch to the wax on his nose, emphasized a line, and then put out the light. Cautiously he went out into the little hall: under his arm he held an attaché-case. In the dark he crept inaudibly towards the pegs on which the coats of the household were hanging. Fumbling at the coats, he singled one out; he felt in the pockets; there were two keys on a ring. He took the coat, and the cap which hung above it, cautiously opened the front door, and stepped out into the street.

He hurried to the Beardmore works; they were only ten minutes distant. He had put on the coat and the cap, and so attired he came to the gate of the works through which his friend was accustomed to pass. Before the gate stood a gatekeeper, smoking his pipe. Graves went straight up to him. He nodded slightly, saying, "I forgot something." The gatekeeper nodded; and next moment Graves was in the Beardmore yard. He had taken his bearings on his previous visit; he had only to turn a few corners, and the door of the one-storied building in which the drawing-office was situated stood open before him. Close to the door sat another watchman, an old man; he was asleep in his chair. As the door creaked on its hinges he woke and looked up. There, in the dim light of the doorway, he saw the familiar figure of the young draughtsman, who called out to him: "I've just got to look for something," and went in. The watchman sank back in his chair, and dozed off again.

Graves went swiftly down a long corridor, turned off to the left, and again to the right, opened the door of the drawing-office, and closed it quietly behind him.

Now he went quickly to work. The great arc-lamp outside the window gave him enough light for the first part of his task; but it made him nervous. He climbed lightly on to the draughtsman's table before the window, and covered the window with a piece of black oilcloth, cut precisely to the right size, which he took from his attaché-case. Then, taking the keys and a flash-lamp from his pocket, he opened the safe, took out the plans, put three of them—the original drawings—on one side, returned the others to the safe, and took off his overcoat.

Taking some drawing-pins from his pocket, he fastened the three drawings on the door. Quickly he glided back. By the light of his pocket-lamp he took a camera from his attaché-case, and quickly and skilfully set it up on the drawing-table. Then, uncovering the lens, he struck a match, and suddenly and silently a little ribbon of magnesium filled the room with a dazzling white radiance. With incredible celerity he repeated the process three times, until all three drawings had been photographed. The dust and smell of the burnt magnesium filled the room. Graves carefully closed the camera, removed the drawings, locked them in the safe, removed the oilcloth from the window, and opened it wide, allowing the fresh air to stream in.

Then he left the office, passing the watchman, who nodded half asleep, passed through the yard into the street, and hurried home. Inaudibly he opened the door; the coat and cap were returned to their pegs, and he disappeared into his room, where he washed the grease-paint from his face, put away his wig, and sitting down before a little red lamp, proceeded to develop the photographs.

On the plates, in perfect definition, every detail visible, the secret plans appeared.

The negatives were printed on very thin paper. Of each plate only one print was made; then the negatives were destroyed.

The prints were placed in a small metal tube, which Graves, as he went to work in the morning, thrust into the soil of the little garden, carefully marking its position. There it was left for a couple of days. And then, at breakfast, on the Sunday, Graves informed his friends that he was going to make a little excursion; he had heard that a countryman of his was living not far from Glasgow.

Soon after breakfast he took his departure. He strolled out of the town and along a country road. There were no pedestrians to be seen; now and again a motor-car passed him; and by the side of the road was a stationary car whose chauffeur was attending to the engine. Graves went slowly up to the car, and then, since there was no one about to notice what he did, he jumped into it. The chauffeur closed the bonnet and climbed into his seat; the car moved off and sped swiftly along the road. After a few miles it stopped. A very well-dressed elderly gentleman, with a grey beard and gold-rimmed spectacles, wearing a thick motoring-coat, descended from the car. Once more there was no one in sight. The chauffeur now got into the closed car. Once more the car ran a few miles, and then stopped. Now a young lady, wrapped in costly furs, stepped out of the car, and gracefully took her seat beside the elderly gentleman, who was driving. And now the car, with its two occupants, raced southwards on the road to London, at the extreme speed of which it was capable.

In a London hotel a young lady was waiting. She sat in an arm-chair, reading a newspaper. A dignified elderly gentleman entered the hotel lounge, accompanied by another young lady.

"Uncle!" cried the lady in the arm-chair. "There you are—and Elizabeth too! I'm so glad you've been able to come! Let's go up to my room."

Upstairs, in the lady's private sitting-room, the uncle was an uncle no longer, but the spy Karl Graves, lately a clockmaker in the employment of a Glasgow cabinet-

79

maker; and his daughter Elizabeth was Miss Mary McCann, a British subject, in the pay of the German Intelligence Service. She acted as the connecting-link between Graves and his paymasters; and the interview took the form of a consultation between a German woman agent from headquarters and Graves and his assistant.

During this consultation Graves delivered the photographs, greatly to the satisfaction of the German woman, and it was decided that in order to expedite the forwarding of information Mary McCann was to settle down in Glasgow; whatever Graves managed to ascertain she could then herself take to Berlin.

Next morning the clockmaker returned to his work, and Miss McCann rented a modest room in Glasgow. In addition to her personal luggage she had a small trunk which contained an extensive collection of sewing-silks. She informed her landlady that she was acting as the English traveller for a large Dutch firm of silk-spinners.

Four times in all the spy paid his perilous visits to the drawing-office, disguised as the young draughtsman. And on the evening after each of his last three visits he went to some little tea-shop and drank a cup of tea; and each time a young lady—apparently a stranger, since the two did not address one another—sat at his table. The lady always left the shop first, taking with her the newspaper which she had been reading.

The lady was Mary McCann, and in the newspaper,

which the spy had exchanged for the one which she had begun by reading, were the photographs.

Graves now made ready to bring off an important *coup*, which would cast into the shade even the brilliant achievements which he already had to his credit. The last time he had visited the Beardmore works in disguise the watchman had called out to ask what was the matter with him, and why he was always going back to the drawing-office after his night shift was over. He had replied to the question with a jest, and the watchman had thought no more about the matter. Still, there was the fact: his visits to the drawing-office had already attracted attention. Graves, therefore, decided to make only one more visit to the works; but this time he proposed to open the doors of the other drawing-offices; he had provided himself with the tools which he would need in order to open the primitive safes; and this time he intended to take no photographs, but to steal the drawings themselves, and bid a hasty farewell to Scotland.

He had not the least suspicion that even as he laid his plans there was someone already on his track.

The British Admiralty was very anxious that the contract which had been awarded to Messrs. Beardmore should be quickly and punctually carried out, so that certain ships, which would shortly be completed, might be equipped with the new guns by a certain date. At the same time, they reflected that the haste with which the work was being pushed forward might result in the firm becoming a little careless in the matter of precautions against spying.

Suddenly, then, Captain Trench appeared in the works. No one realized that he was there, and he was given quite a subordinate post; he was appointed inspector of the gatekeepers, cleaners and night-watchmen. He had to see that the workmen and the subordinate employés were punctual in coming to their work; in short, he was given a place which gave him the right to poke his nose into everything.

He had already entered upon his duties when Graves, disguised as the young draughtsman, paid his fourth visit to the works. Nothing escaped Trench; and so, early one morning, he learned from the gatekeeper that nothing particular had happened in the night; there was nothing to report at all, apart from the unimportant fact that a draughtsman who had forgotten something had just run back to his office during the night.

Trench inquired whether it was possible for him to do so as simply as all that; and who was in charge of the keys of the different doors of the drawing-offices? He learned that the doors were never locked at night; and then he inquired as to the identity of the draughtsman in question. Finally it came out that during the last month this man had returned to the works, during the small hours of the morning, no less than four times.

Trench lit his pipe, saying: "Oh, well, why shouldn't he?" and walked away.

But he was privately convinced that there was something queer about this business of the forgetful draughtsman. Accordingly he himself went to the drawing-office. The charwomen had not yet made their appearance. He went into the room in which the turner's son had his drawing-table.

Trench had only been a few seconds in the room before he realized what had happened. He sniffed the air, and noted the slight taint of burned magnesium; he lay on his stomach and searched all over the floor until he found a few fragments of a white filmy substance, and he knew that these were the ashes of a piece of magnesium ribbon.

Now he thoroughly inspected the whole room. He found a number of tiny holes in the surface of the door, and these told a man of his experience almost the whole story. The draughtsman who had such a bad memory had been photographing drawings during his nocturnal visits.

At first Trench did nothing at all. It seemed as though he had no intention of pursuing the matter. But about this time Graves received information, through Miss McCann, to the effect that a commission of inspection had arrived in Glasgow for the purpose of taking over the guns and control machinery which Messrs. Beardmore had been manufacturing. The members of the commission were naval officers and engineers, and they had with them plans relating to important armaments, the contract for which would possibly be given to Beardmore's.

About this time too the draughtsman came home one day with the news that all the drawing-offices were being removed, and in the course of the conversation Graves learned that for the time being all original plans and drawings of importance had been transferred to the safe in his friend's room. They would be there for a couple of days, until the alterations were completed. Almost at the same time Graves learned from Mary McCann that German agents in London had reported to Berlin that Captain Trench, one of the best of the English spies, had been sent to Glasgow. It was known that he would be there for some time, but nothing was known of his purpose.

That night Karl Graves found it difficult to sleep. The thought of all the drawings which were now in his friend's safe was terribly fascinating. But why had Trench suddenly come to Glasgow? He knew the man by name, and he knew, too, that he was an exceptionally clever agent. And suddenly enlightenment came to him. Wasn't there perhaps an essential connection between the two things? Instinctively he felt that he was on the right track. And he concocted a plan by which he could arrive at certainty.

In the Beardmore works matters had now resumed their normal course. The double shifts had been discontinued, and now his friend, together with his officemate, was working only by day. The two draughtsmen whom they had been relieving had been transferred to some other department.

One evening, after the draughtsman had returned from his day's work, the clockmaker suddenly recollected that his employer had asked him to make a few drawings for the clockmaker's workshop. It turned out that he had forgotten his compasses; the workshop was a good way off, and it was a fine evening; in short, he asked the draughtsman if he could just oblige him by running back to the works to get his compasses?

It was then about eight o'clock. Three hours later the draughtsman had not yet returned. All the inmates of the turner's house had long been asleep in their beds when Karl Graves quietly left the house with all his possessions, never again to enter it.

That which he had feared and foreseen had happened. The young draughtsman had passed the night-watchman and gone into the drawing-office, but even as he went up to his desk to take out the compasses the door of the room opened, a man came up to him, showed him his authority, and arrested him.

The draughtsman was flabbergasted. Captain Trench and two of the directors of the works interrogated him; they wanted to know what he had been doing in the drawing-office during his four previous nocturnal visits. The draughtsman gazed uncomprehendingly at his questioners. He had never once returned to the works during the night; he did not understand what was wanted of him; and even when confronted by the gate-keeper and the night-watchman of the drawing-office he persisted in his denial.

While the directors were convinced that the draughtsman was lying, an idea suddenly occurred to Captain Trench. He asked the young man, who had more than once burst out crying during the interrogation, to explain precisely why it was that he had returned to the works that night. When he heard the draughts-man's story of the Swiss clockmaker and the compasses he stopped short, telephoned secretly for a couple of policemen, and then—it being by now about midnight —he went to the draughtsman's house in order to have a look at the clockmaker. When he found that the bird had flown he could roughly guess what had happened.

But Karl Graves too had been thinking over the events of the evening. When the draughtsman did not at once return he put two and two together; evidently something was already suspected, and the young man was being interrogated. But any interrogation would inevitably elicit the fact of his existence. To avoid the consequences of that discovery he hastily made his escape.

Meanwhile the commission already mentioned had put up at the Central Hotel. One day a new guest arrived from London: a baldish, corpulent, elderly Dutchman, who engaged a room for a few days. He was a most amiable old gentleman: a Dutch solicitor, who had business in Glasgow. He conversed a good deal with the hotel porter and the waiters, tipped the servants well, and was generally liked.

Captain Trench was in the meanwhile very far from pleased with himself. He was the more discontented in that the British agents in Berlin informed him that a German spy in Glasgow was supposed to have learned all manner of important details relating to the new guns. In Berlin there were all sorts of whispered rumours as to what had occurred; amongst other things, it was said that the secrets which the German spy in Glasgow had discovered had been brought to Berlin by a woman; indeed, that she had brought the original documents. Captain Trench cursed himself when he realized that the spy had slipped through his fingers; for he was convinced that the young draughtsman—who was kept in custody a while for safety—was absolutely innocent.

Trench now began to keep a watch on the members of the Admiralty commission; for he felt sure that the German spy, if he happened still to be in Glasgow, would never be able to leave this commission alone.

He now led a double life. Part of his time he spent as an overseer in the Beardmore works; the rest of the time he spent in the Central Hotel, disguised as a German business man. He secretly studied the signatures of all the guests in the hotel; he studied the people themselves, and three or four of them—and among them the Dutchman—seemed to him possibly suspicious. But he could not put his finger on anything definite.

He then revealed his identity to the manager of the hotel.

In the early hours of the following morning the Dutchman was awakened in his bedroom, which over-looked the street, by the jingle of a broken window-pane. He jumped out of bed, ran to the window, and saw that a telescopic ladder, like a fire-escape, had been set up against the hotel. A man was climbing up the ladder, which was close to the Dutchman's windows, carrying some tools in his hand. He called out an apology to the Dutchman: he had to do some work on the roof, and apparently he had struck the window with his tools, and so had broken the pane. Shortly afterwards there was a knock on the bedroom door. The hotel porter appeared with apologies. A sheet of zinc had got loose on the roof, and was threatening to fall into the street. They had sent for a ladder, and a man had been sent up to make all fast again. But the silly fellow had broken the window with his tools. The Dutchman muttered something and went back to bed.

Next morning, after breakfast, he was sitting in the hotel lounge reading the newspaper. A page-boy came to tell him that he was wanted on the telephone. He stood up and went towards the telephone-box, and as he turned into a corridor two men suddenly seized him. They bent his arms backwards, and he felt handcuffs on his wrists. Captain Trench pulled the Dutchman's wig off his head, smiled a satisfied smile, and put it in his pocket.

"You know," he said, "what was the meaning of that business with the broken window? I just wanted to see whether you had black hair at night."

He then left the prisoner in charge of the two detectives, and went into the telephone-box to which Graves had been summoned.

"Hullo!" he said.

A voice answered: "Is that you, Graves?"

"Yes: Graves speaking."

A feminine voice continued: "It's Mary. When are you going to meet me?"

Trench replied: "I'll come at once, but tell me, where am I to meet you?"

"What do you mean?" said the woman's voice. "You wrote me where I am to meet you."

"Of course I did," said Trench, "but I must confess, to my shame, that I've forgotten the place!"

Mary McCann reminded him; and Trench replied that he would come at once.

But it was not Graves who entered the café where Mary McCann was waiting; it was Trench, and he brought with him quite a number of detectives. He was lucky: there were only two customers in the café, a man and a woman; and since the woman had papers on her from which it appeared that her Christian name was Mary, he arrested her.

Captain Trench was unable to extract an admission from Graves that it was he who had on four several nights taken photographs in Messrs. Beardmore's drawing-office. And the spy's luggage furnished no evidence of any sort until his leather trunk was picked to pieces. Between the sides and the lining an abundance of material was found. To begin with, there were several pages of thin, closely-written paper, on which the dimensions and other details of the new guns were carefully recorded. And a little tube was found which contained a dose of a virulent poison; and finally, a small pocket-book. Several pages of this pocket-book were gummed together, and on the concealed pages was a telegraphic code. Similar things were found in the possession of Mary McCann, and, accompanied by the lady, Captain Trench made the rounds of all the telegraph-offices in Glasgow. At several of these offices the officials remembered Miss McCann. The originals of her telegrams were looked up, and it was found that they contained series of numbers, incorporated in a harmless-looking message. These telegrams were sent to Holland, and they bore a signature which in itself would never have aroused suspicion—the signature of the well-known firm of Messrs. Burroughs, Wellcome & Co.

Graves was brought up for trial in July, 1912, Mary McCann appearing as witness. He was accused of having communicated information relating to the British fleet and the land defences to the German Government by means of a code. Further, he was believed to have discovered and communicated the secret details of the guns then being made by Messrs. William Beardmore & Co., of Glasgow. Admiral Stratton Adair had succeeded in deciphering the code. It contained code signs for almost every vessel in the British Navy, and such complex contingencies, for example, as the sailing of a squadron composed of certain units were represented by groups of figures. These figures, however, were not read as they were written and telegraphed, but first of all the number 271 had to be subtracted from the total sum. It was an uncommonly clever code, and very carefully thought out.

Graves's bearing throughout the trial was that of a cultured gentleman. The President of the Court, Lord Justice Clerk Macdonald, was openly sympathetic in his attitude to the prisoner. The sentence was a lenient one. Graves was condemned to eighteen months' imprisonment. If Trench had been able to prove that he had photographed the plans in Messrs. Beardmore's drawing-office he would have received a very different sentence.

Graves then was removed to prison to serve his sentence. When he had been in prison a few days he asked permission to write a letter to Captain Trench. He received the desired permission, and Trench received a letter in which Graves begged the captain to pay him a visit.

Trench accordingly went to see him. Graves explained that he had conceived the greatest respect for the brilliant work of the British Intelligence Service. And for some time he had been dissatisfied with the way in which the German Intelligence Service had been treating him. If after his release he were now to return to Germany he would simply be thrown on the scrap-heap. He had no idea what he would do. Did Trench feel inclined to make use of him?

Trench listened to his offer, and reflected. He knew that Graves was an able man, and to begin with, at all events, the Germans would not suspect him; but he did not know whether he ought to accept the offer.

Then Graves sprang a surprise on him. Trench

paid him another visit, and during this second interview the German hinted that he knew that certain important military and political negotiations between Germany and Japan were then proceeding in America. These negotiations had been projected before his arrest, and even the date, which was now approaching, had been settled. Graves gave the names of the persons who would conclude the proposed agreement, and he even named the steamer by which, on a given date, a German diplomatist would sail for New York.

Captain Trench telegraphed to his agents in New York and Berlin. The replies told him that the Japanese whom Graves had named were actually staying in the hotel which he had indicated, and that cabins had really been reserved for certain German diplomatists on the steamer in question. Trench now believed the German's story; and so it came about that a few days later Karl Graves, beaming with delight, walked out of his prison a free man. He had pledged himself to proceed at once to New York, in order to ascertain the details of the proposed military agreement between Japan and Germany, and to betray them to the English. Captain Trench himself accompanied him on board the steamer by which he was to sail for New York.

It was an English boat, so that Graves did not feel that he was really free until he leaped ashore on the neutral soil of the United States. He then wrote down and sent to Captain Trench what he believed were the terms of the agreement concluded between Germany and Japan. With this he felt that he had done his best to repay the consideration which had been shown him; and he then disappeared for ever.

CHAPTER FIVE

THIS is the story of the greatest of the German women spies, who served Germany both during the war and before it. Her real name, and indeed her very existence, was long concealed: only a few people knew that there was such a person, and only after the war did Colonel Nikolai make a passing mention of her in his book *Geheime Mächte*. He said of her that apart from a certain specially appointed officer the person best qualified to deal with secret service agents was a handsome and remarkably clever woman. Hers is a fantastic story, and she came to a terrible end. She was known as "Mademoiselle docteur"—the "lady doctor"—to enemy spies and agents; her real name was Annemarie Lesser, and her parents' house was in the Tiergartenstrasse in Berlin. At the age of sixteen she fell in love with Carl von Wynanky, a captain of the Guard Hussars. As her connection with him was not without consequences, her father turned her out of the house, and she gave birth to a dead child. Captain von Wynanky resigned from the Hussars, but was later recalled to the colours, and appointed captain in a railway battalion. He was ambitious, and assiduous in his duties, for he hoped to be

transferred to the General Staff. His mistress, Annemarie Lesser, was at this time living in Berlin; she had
made no definite plans as to her future, and was living
on the money which the captain sent her. And then
disaster overtook Carl von Wynanky. The family
estate, which was administered by his brothers, was
encumbered with debt; his monthly allowance was
greatly reduced, and, such as it was, it was largely
pledged to his creditors. In short, he was in a desperate
condition. His commanding officer insisted that he must
either pay his debts or send in his papers. In his
extremity he went to Berlin, to consult a former comrade who was now a lieutenant-colonel on the Great
General Staff. The colonel arranged an interview between the captain and a distinguished officer of high
rank who was already known to him, and this officer
referred him to a certain Matthesius, who had an office
in Bülowstrasse. This office, which to all appearances
was that of an ordinary dealer in motor-cars and acces-
sories, was actually an intelligence bureau. The captain
was quite prepared, if only he could pay his debts, and
continue to provide for Annemarie Lesser, to act as a
spy in the interests of his Fatherland; and one day,
after his debts had been paid, and he had received his
discharge from the Army, he met Herr J. Matthesius
in the restaurant of the Hôtel Adlon. Herr Matthesius
was small and emaciated; his prominent cheek-bones
were framed in mutton-chop whiskers; under his pro-
jecting brows were two restless little eyes; and his bony,

angular figure was clad in a remarkably well-cut blue lounge suit.

"This is what you have to do," began Matthesius curtly, and without preliminaries: "To-day is Wednesday. To-night you will go to Paris by the night express. In Paris you will go to the offices of Meunier & Co., whose address is on this slip. You will commit the address to memory, and destroy the slip. Meunier & Co. are quite a young firm; they are obliged to be economical, and at present they have no clerks. They are handling ball-bearings for motor-cars, pneumatic tyres, and so on, and they are in business relations with my own firm. Now, a man has come to these people with the offer of the plans of an automatic gun, a field-gun, capable of enormously rapid fire: probably more or less on the lines of a revolver. You are a soldier; you must know something of these things. The price asked for the plans is five thousand marks. You will take this money with you, in cash, and you will buy the plans if you are convinced of their value. But you will buy them only if you have personally ascertained that the French military authorities have already accepted these plans, and are preparing to construct guns of this type. You will not telegraph; you will not write; but when you have concluded your business, in a negative or a positive sense, you will return to Berlin, and ring me up. We will then arrange to meet somewhere. This is a serious business, captain, and if you don't pull it off it's the last time I shall have to address you by that title. Here is a cheque for your expense. And now, au revoir!"

In Paris, von Wynanky climbed up the steep stairs to the office of Meunier & Co. The sole representative of the firm, an extraordinarily taciturn person, for he scarcely uttered a word, introduced von Wynanky that evening, in a small café, to a rather scrubby-looking individual, who thought that he had now been dealing quite long enough with Messieurs Meunier; he would wait another twenty-four hours, and then someone else would get the drawings. The captain pulled himself together; he took charge of the negotiations, curtly took his leave of Monsieur Pissard, the representative of Meunier & Co., and took the scrubby-looking man to his hotel. Here he saw the drawings, and examined them for a couple of hours. Smoking one cigarette after another, the Frenchman sat and waited, and finally agreed to return about the same time on the following evening.

That same night Wynanky pulled Monsieur Pissard out of his bed and insisted that he must give him, then and there, a certificate, with photograph, to the effect that he was employed by Messieurs Meunier & Co. in the capacity of engineer; and by the following day he must have a passport for Switzerland, made out in any name but his own, with an accurate description of his person. "I have got the photographs here; I thought in Berlin that something of the sort might be required." —Monsieur Pissard was taken aback. He assured the German that such a thing could not be done as quickly as he seemed to think. It would require at least a week. Wynanky sat on the edge of the Frenchman's bed, puzzling his brains as to what he had better do next. Suddenly an idea struck him.

"Well," he said, "they told me you were an experienced man; they told me you understood our trade. Don't you think the people in Berlin will be rather astonished when they learn that their Paris agent is a downright ass, an accursed idiot? What do you imagine we pay you for? To tell me that you can't get me a false passport at a few hours' notice?"

Monsieur Pissard flung himself over in his bed, and buried his face in the pillows. Wynanky assumed that the Frenchman was abashed by his violent rebukes. He would have been greatly astonished if he had known that the man in the bed was doing his utmost to suppress a satisfied smile.

Captain von Wynanky received his passport. It informed him that his name was now George Nieweg, and he greatly admired the faultless reproduction of the official stamp on the paper. And then he did something which, when it was known in the world of international agents, was the cause of great amusement; he went, gaily and cheerfully, straight into the lion's den, to the headquarters of the French General Staff, and there he exhibited the plans of the automatic gun to the engineer captain on duty. His excellent memory had helped him. During the night he had reproduced the plans of the scrubby stranger. The engineer officer pushed back the papers at the first glance.

"You tell me you are a technical expert, and you waste your spare time on that sort of thing! My dear sir, take my advice, and go fishing, or play football, or increase the population, but don't waste your time on ridiculous plans like that. The thing would explode by the second shot."

"Of course it would!" said the captain, in silence, to himself. He had a very dejected expression as he took his leave of the Frenchman.

On the following day, an hour after the arrival of the Paris express in Berlin, Wynanky was closeted with Herr J. Matthesius.

"I saw at once," he said, "that the plans were mere rubbish. If you are going to fire so many shots, at such a rate, out of one barrel, you must have some very different method of cooling the barrel. As a matter of fact, no system of cooling would suffice; and secondly, there is as yet no system of glycerine recoil-chambers that would stand up to such firing; but just to make sure I asked the French captain of engineers at head-quarters——"

"Excuse me," said Matthesius, thoroughly startled, "but whom did you ask?"

"Whom? I've told you, the technical expert on the French General Staff," and he told Matthesius precisely what had passed between them.

Matthesius looked at his watch, and discovered that he had an important appointment. He requested the captain to put up somewhere in Berlin for the time being, and to telephone the address to his office.

That evening Matthesius and Pissard had an interview.

"I have come specially from Paris," said Pissard, "simply to tell you that you have got the very devil of a fellow in this Wynanky. I don't mind betting you that he saw that these plans were rubbish at the very first glance. Do you know that he went to the French General Staff? If he told you that he was telling the truth; I followed him. The man has passed the test brilliantly, and now we can begin to use him. But for goodness' sake be careful; for if he ever learns that we've been playing a little comedy with him to test him, then the Lord have mercy upon me. Unless I am mistaken, he is very much stronger than I am."

That evening Wynanky was sitting by the bedside of his mistress. Annemarie Lesser was ill. There was nothing definite the matter with her, but the prospect of continuing to live without him was filling her with despair, and the captain saw that unless he could bring about a complete change in her way of life the results would be disastrous. During the night an idea occurred to him. Five days later, when Matthesius asked him to follow the course of the Meuse from Sorcy to Dinant, and to pay particular attention to certain specified details, he took Annemarie with him. But in Strasbourg, when Wynanky, after a severe internal conflict, told his mistress what he was actually doing, he found that his troubles were by no means ended. Annemarie, horrified at the thought of the perils of his occupation, broke into hysterical weeping; but she soon recovered her equanimity, and a week later, when the two were walking or driving down the course of the river, the girl was quite reconciled to her new situation. The fact that she would no longer be separated from her lover made up for everything.

Some weeks later Matthesius received the most accurate sketches of the new fortifications of the Meuse fortresses, and detailed plans of the existing and newly surveyed strategic railways, which were not marked on any of the maps of the district.

Some little time later the two spies proceeded to Charleville, with detailed instructions. "Where does the line of the first field fortifications on the Charleville-Verdun sector begin, travelling from north to south? Where are its strong and where its weak points?" And this time Annemarie Lesser understood precisely what was required of her, and Wynanky found that her knowledge of the French language, acquired in a good Swiss boarding-school, was quite equal to his own. He discovered, with delight which was not unmixed with dismay, that Annemarie had a way of her own with peasants, postmen, railway officials and what not; these simple folk were so delighted with her that they would tell her anything she asked them. Now that she was always with her lover she soon learned the essentials of her new calling; she was quick to understand what sort of information was required—and how to acquire it. Many weeks of that hot summer were spent by the lovers in wandering through the countryside between Charleville and Verdun. Wynanky, who was now George Nieweg, with a Swiss passport, always carried a rucksack, which contained books on botany, and a herbarium, and the simple implements of the botanist.

One night they were sleeping in the little inn of a small French village when Annemarie woke, and roused her lover. "We have been followed!" she whispered. Her heart was throbbing as though it would burst. She found it impossible to sleep again. She got quietly out of bed, and peeped out of the window, and was so restless and terrified that she infected her lover with her uneasiness; so the next morning they drove to Charleville and there took tickets for Cologne. After all, they had finished their task; in the lining of Wynanky's waistcoat were many thin sheets of closely written paper, covered with figures and symbols.

The train was due in a quarter of an hour; the lovers were waiting on the platform of the Charleville railway station. Suddenly Annemarie saw in front of her a man in a well-cut grey suit, with a scrap of red ribbon in his button-hole; a man whom she had seen four times in the course of the last week. A few days earlier —she realized it now—he had been wearing a forester's uniform, and she had spoken to him and questioned him. And she knew now that only the night before she had seen him in the barroom of the little inn, dressed as a farm labourer. And after that she had waked with the feeling that they were being watched. . . .

The man was looking about him. He could not see Wynanky and the girl; they happened at the moment to be standing behind a mail-van. Silently Annemarie gripped her lover's hand. He looked into her face; it was as white as a sheet. Now both of them were looking at the man, and Wynanky, too, recognized him. They saw him speaking to five other men; and then he went through the booking-hall to the barrier; and then—still peering from their chance hiding-place— they saw two men, tall and thick-set, armed with heavy-knobbed sticks, station themselves inconspicuously by the barrier, as though to keep watch on those who passed through. The man with the red ribbon in his button-hole returned to the platform, and the five men to whom he had previously spoken strolled off to one end of the station, and then, walking very slowly, proceeded to patrol the platform. So far they could not see behind the mail-cart; but what when they came nearer? Then Annemarie made up her mind. She whispered a few words to her lover, and he, without more ado, followed her, slowly approaching the barrier from the left. And there at the barrier stood the two men with the heavy sticks. But Annemarie, approaching the barrier from the right, suddenly and swiftly came up to the two men, and seizing one of them by the lapels of his coat, hissed out the words: "Quick— I've been sent to fetch you—I'm an agent of the Sûreté —they've caught the woman spy, and the man—they are resisting—they have revolvers!"

"Thanks!" said the man. He took just one quick and benevolent look at this handsome young woman, who was obviously a good Frenchwoman, and rushed off with his comrade; and as they ran out on to the platform the lovers quietly passed through the barrier. Once outside the station they moved more quickly: in a moment they jumped into a landau, and set out at a trot "for a drive in the country." In the first village they came to they paid the driver, took a short walk across country, found another carriage, and then—just as the warning telegrams were beginning to reach the village *maires*—a motor-car, which took them over the Belgian frontier; and at last they came to Charleroi, where they took the express for Cologne. The German frontier was crossed; the lovers were safe; and then Wynanky confessed that ever since the morning he had been suffering the most terrible internal pain.

Groaning with agony, he climbed out of the train at Cologne. He could not walk; he drove to St. Vincent's hospital; and that very night a pitiless Fate set a period to Annemarie Lesser's romance. For during the night the ex-captain Carl von Wynanky died of perforating appendicitis, and his young mistress was left alone, helpless and beside herself with grief.

The hospital authorities learned from Annemarie the address of the dead officer's family. And Annemarie herself remembered that her lover had impressed upon her that if anything ever happened to him she must without a moment's delay send word to a Herr J. Matthesius in Bülowstrasse, Berlin.

Telegrams were soon flying in all directions. In the Dom Hotel Annemarie met her lover's relatives on their arrival. She went up to the dead man's brother, and asked him when the funeral would take place; she was told that it was no concern of hers, and that the family begged her not to show herself at the grave of the man for whose misfortune she was responsible. The Wynanky family knew nothing of the captain's recent exploits; they were convinced that he had "gone to the dogs," and that it was Annemarie who had "dragged him down."

Annemarie was weeping helplessly in her room when an officer of the Cologne garrison made his appearance: a pleasant and tactful young man, who explained that he was instructed to ask Annemarie for the dead man's papers. Annemarie sprang to her feet; in her misery she had not given a thought to his papers; they were sewed into the dead man's waistcoat. And so, while the family were assembled in the chapel of the hospital, round the coffin in which the dead man lay, dressed in the suit which he had worn on the last day of his life, an officer came forward, accompanied by a few civilians. "By order of the general commanding! The body is sequestrated!"

The family were startled and astounded; they understood, and could understand, nothing; however, half an hour before the time of the funeral the body was released for burial. That evening the tactful lieutenant again visited Annemarie. At first she refused to open her door; she could not and would not see or speak to anyone; she wanted only to follow her lover to the grave. But the officer spoke and spoke through the closed door, and at last Annemarie opened it; and the first thing the officer did on entering the room was to pocket a small revolver which he saw lying on the table. The lieutenant accompanied her to the railway station; he requested her on her arrival in Berlin to go straight to a Herr Matthesius, whose address he gave her. During the journey to Berlin the girl pulled herself together. At the terminus she was met by a skinny little man who proved to be none other than Matthesius, and who begged her to accompany him. He had recognized her at once: "a young lady in deep mourning." On his office table lay the closely-written sheets which had been found in the dead man's waistcoat, and beside them some maps, a pair of compasses, and paper. Annemarie quickly composed herself; she began to explain the dead man's notes, to point out positions on the maps. These figures on the left of Wynanky's notes referred to the squares of the maps of the General Staff; these lines were strategic railways, those were trenches; these positions were occupied during the last manœuvres; and so on, and so on. Matthesius whistled through his teeth. For hours the two transferred the notes to a map of the frontier district; clearly and precisely Annemarie continued her explanations, while the bony little man sketched away in silence, and when all was done, and the dawn was breaking, he pressed Annemarie's hand, and said:

"How do you do it all? I think we must have another talk to-morrow."

Annemarie slept on a sofa, in Matthesius' house, and cried in her sleep.

While she was still sleeping two men were walking down a lonely path in the Tiergarten. One was Matthesius; the other was a gentleman whom he addressed as "Excellency."

HIS EXCELLENCY: "I think your proposal is perfectly grotesque. The fact that the girl can decipher poor Wynanky's notes, and explain them, doesn't prove that she could ascertain such things for herself."

MATTHESIUS: "I know something of my fellow creatures. At all events, I am in favour of giving her one trial. Besides, I'm sorry for the poor young thing. . . ."

HIS EXCELLENCY: "If you are sorry for the girl, let her earn her living as a governess or school teacher; one can't send a girl as young as that into such danger."

MATTHESIUS: "She won't go out of her way to avoid danger. We shall see that I'm right."

HIS EXCELLENCY: "Well, do as you will; after all, you ought to know."

That afternoon, pale and tearful, Annemarie sat facing Matthesius. The thin little man began to speak. His slender, well-kept hands glided over the maps, played with the compasses, scribbled aimlessly on the paper.

"What do you propose to do now?" he asked.

"I don't know. Nothing."

"But you'll have to do something."

"I shall just make an end of myself."

"Do you think that is what your dead friend would have wished you to do?"

"Then I should like to do something that would be so exacting that I should forget all about myself."

There was a pause. Matthesius fidgeted with his maps.

Then Annemarie spoke. "Couldn't I perhaps . . . ?"

"Of course you can, if you like. Listen to me. You will go into the Vosges. You will ascertain this and that . . ."

Once more they sat together, poring over the maps and the official publications of the French Army, until the dawn was breaking. The girl's weary eyes began to sparkle with life; she challenged the little man's statements, she made suggestions, she rejected this or that proposal, and made others of her own. Matthesius grew hot and excited, but they finally came to an agreement, and shook hands on it.

On the following day Annemarie took a room in a hotel.

Some days later a young girl—apparently about sixteen—arrived, with her trunks and hat-boxes, at a boarding-house in Bismarckstrasse, Charlottenburg. Two long pigtails hung down her back. Fortunately, Annemarie was small and slender.

Matthesius escorted the girl to the station, and saw her into the Colmar express. From a distance an old gentleman watched the girl as she boarded the train. After the train had left the old gentleman met Matthesius on the steps before the station. "You are perfectly crazy. The girl is a mere child!"

Matthesius went quietly down the steps. To all

appearances the old gentleman who was descending the steps at his side was a stranger to him, but he was muttering to himself as he left the station, and the old gentleman caught the words: "Just you wait, your Excellency!"

It was a beautiful sunny autumn day when Annemarie Lesser, an art student from Geneva, arrived in a village of the French Vosges. Her passport, with its Swiss stamp and *visa*, stated that she was sixteen years of age; and in her boarding-house she soon became the pet of the guests and servants alike. Every day she went for a long walk in the hills. Wherever she went she quickly made friends; the foresters helped her to set up the tripod of her camera; the railway officials complained to her of their long hours of exacting service; and the *gardes champêtres* directed her on her way, telling her of roads and footpaths which would shortly be improved, and of new roads which were projected.

One evening, when she returned to her boarding-house, she found the whole village in commotion. A division of troops on manœuvres had marched into the place, and had to be billeted there. She had read of manœuvres in the local newspapers, and they were, of course, mentioned in the Paris newspapers, and also in the German press. That evening Annemarie sat beside an old hard-bitten captain, surrounded by younger officers, and, of course, by her fellow-guests; there was dancing that night, and a good deal of wine was drunk, and on the following morning the troops marched off to their manœuvres. Following them in a little chaise, drawn by the plump, glossy little horse of the boarding-house keeper, who was well paid for its hire, was Anne-marie Lesser, the sixteen-year-old art student. She had been invited by the captain.

Divisional manœuvres! — Annemarie knew the strength of the French divisions, and she saw, at the first glance, that more than a whole army corps was in the field. Before leaving Berlin she had carefully read the announcements of the great manœuvres of the French Army, and she realized at once that there was an enormous discrepancy between the official announce-ment and the manœuvres which she was now observing.

"I have never seen any cannon before!" said Anne-marie; and that evening the worthy captain escorted her through the artillery positions.

Annemarie was indefatigable; day after day she fol-lowed the troops in her little chaise. The soldiers soon got to know her; it was a pleasure to see the pretty young girl who was dressed in such gay colours; and the elderly captain began to strut like a peacock, for Annemarie was continually taking his photograph in some fresh pose, and it never occurred to the officer that there was always some battery or trench system in the background. How should he notice such things? He had eyes only for this delightful child, and one eve-ning, before the end of the manœuvres, under a per-fectly romantic lime-tree, he made her a proposal of marriage. Annemarie had only one objection to make.

"What does an officer's wife do with herself? Tell me what your duties are!" And the enamoured captain plunged into all sorts of details. He was a genuine "ranker" officer, a soldier of experience; he had worked his way up from the rank of corporal, and knew nothing of anything outside his profession. It was a pleasure to him to talk of these things with a beautiful young girl; though it was not easy for an old soldier to explain all the latest innovations. "They dig everything in nowadays; and the sights are differently divided, and the area of fire is different; and one has to keep up with all these things. In the old days it used to be so and so; but now. . . ."

When the east winds began to blow Annemarie decided that she must go home to consult her mother, and the captain at once hired a good car for her, and an orderly officer and a sergeant escorted the little lady, with her trunks, sketch books and camera, to the frontier. There was no inspection of her luggage by the customs; the sergeant explained to the customs officials that he did not wish his captain's fiancée to be put to any trouble; and the photographs, which were not yet developed, remained intact, for Annemarie had explained to the sergeant that they were particularly important; she must be able to send the captain his photographs.

Annemarie, in order to be provided for all contingencies, took a ticket for Geneva; but before she reached that city she changed into the Berlin express.

In the sleeping-car she lay long awake, and when at

last she fell asleep she was smiling; she felt that Wynanky would have been contented with her.

On the following day Matthesius, when he came to his office, was almost beside himself.

"The French artillery is no longer made with the open mounting? It is armoured up to the muzzle, even in case of a war of manœuvre? Who has been making a fool of you? These are sketches of earthworks that you have brought me here, and you ask me to believe that in future they will make such trenches for fighting in open country?"

"Give me a cigarette. I am getting quite accustomed to smoking; don't be alarmed, only when I am alone. It would hardly be fitting at my official age!— Well, so you think they have been making a fool of me? Then what do you say to these photographs?"

Matthesius was silent for a while; finally he whistled through his teeth. "This is positively sensational," he said quietly. "I will be frank with you—this is the most important discovery that has been made for years. We Germans are still refusing to fit armoured screens to our guns; and these fellows here are digging themselves in up to their noses! This is a tremendous business!"

Four days later Annemarie rang up Matthesius. "I can't bear it any longer; I can't live without work. Where shall I go now?"

"Beverloo!" said Matthesius.

After her success in the Vosges Annemarie received a regular salary from Matthesius; she was given a number by which other agents might know her, and which she was to use, in case of emergency, if she had to call up her employer. She was "one and four, G and W." That winter she remained in Berlin. Together with Matthesius she went through all the secret information concerning the military armaments of foreign countries; she was an apt pupil and a diligent worker. She made the personal acquaintance of the more important secret agents, with whom she might one day have to co-operate in places less safe than Berlin. In the spring of 1914 she made her long-postponed journey to Belgium. Her task was to examine the country around the little town of St. Sebastian, and the great manœuvring ground of Beverloo, close to the Dutch frontier. In addition to this she had to obtain the statistics of the armaments of the great Belgian fortresses. How many guns of position were there in the fortifications of Liège? What was their calibre? How was the water regulated in the Belgian rivers and canals, and what tracts of land could be flooded in case of war? What was the condition of the railways?

In the beautiful winter gardens of the Hôtel Anglais in Brussels some Belgian officers had ordered a dinner to celebrate some festive occasion. That same evening Annemarie Lesser entered the dining-room of the hotel. Her name did not appear in the hotel register; she now had a French name, and was provided with a French passport, from which it appeared that she was a native of Paris. That evening a young Belgian lieutenant, René Austin, was passing through

the dining-room, and as he passed Annemarie's table a
glass fell jingling to the floor. The handsome young
woman who had dropped the glass, in whom few would
have recognized the girl who had followed the French
manœuvres in the Vosges, uttered a slight exclamation
of pain. She had cut her hand, and a little drop of
blood had fallen on the yellow damask of the table-
cloth. René Austin was a well-bred and chivalrous
young man. He hurried to her side and escorted her
out of the dining-room. He procured a scrap of lint
and a strip of plaster, and presently the two were comfortably esconced in two of the capacious arm-chairs in
the lounge.

"A broken glass brings luck!" said René Austin.

"Let us hope so!" smiled Annemarie.

The young officer learned that his new acquaintance
was an artist, and that she intended to stay in the
Belgian capital until the summer, studying and copying
the pictures in the great museums.

The young people met in the Musée Wiertz; but
they also met in the Bois de la Cambre. They quickly
became more intimate, and before long René Austin,
whose duties were not very exacting, was spending all
his leisure hours in the company of the handsome art
student.

His new friend was an enthusiastic French patriot,
and cherished a fanatical hatred of the Germans. Her
father, who had long been dead, was an officer of the
French Army, and his daughter had inherited his love
of the soldier's calling. The great and glorious army

of the French nation was something to be proud of!
And what of the Belgian Army? That, of course,.
could not be compared with the French!

"Oh, but we are not so bad!" protested the young
man. "We have this and that and the other. . . ."

For a week Annemarie disappeared. The young
soldier was disconsolate. Then, suddenly, she reappeared. She had been into the country, sketching and
painting. She showed Austin a few charming pen-
drawings; catkin-covered willows on a hill, a barge on a
canal, and so forth; but there were quite a number of
things which she did not show him. To her address
in Berlin she had sent a whole packing-case full of oil
paintings; of a horse on a heath, a windmill, a wooded
landscape, and other subjects. These pictures were
presently unpacked by Matthesius. Quite disregardful
of their artistic merits, he scraped the paint from the
canvas, and under it found drawings which had a much
greater interest for him.

One afternoon a smart little two-seater stood before
the hotel; a car of the very latest type. Annemarie
had just bought it. Austin was a good driver. She
wanted to see more of the countryside.

Austin, head over ears in love, applied for a week's
leave, and drove off with the young Parisian. They
began by going all over the Beverloo district. Annemarie, as an officer's daughter, was keenly interested,
and asked her companion a thousand questions. Then
they visited some of the fortresses, and scrambled
through the casemates and covered ways, to which

Austin, as an officer of the Belgian Army, had no difficulty in obtaining admission. On the sixth day they
drove along the Dutch frontier. Suddenly the car came
to a standstill. Austin opened the bonnet and examined
the engine; Annemarie, producing a little notebook,
tore out a leaf, and asked:

"How much benzine have we used, and how far have
we come? I'll just write it down."

Just as Austin had completed some trifling repair,
Annemarie tried to return the leaf to the notebook, but
in her haste she dropped the leaf; the wind caught it
and carried it away, and Austin ran after it, trying to
catch it.

"No!" cried Annemarie. "Never mind that scrap
of paper!"—but the young officer continued to run after
it as it floated, eddying over the road and the adjacent
meadow. Annemarie ran after it too; perhaps she could
catch it first. The paper was wafted into a drainage-
trench. Austin jumped down after it, and for a little
while he was invisible to Annemarie; there was a hedge
between them. It was some time before he returned
to the road. Then he said: "The paper is lost; it fell
into a pool." They returned to the car, and Austin
pressed the accelerator. The car tore along the high-
way. Annemarie took a sidelong glance at her companion. Austin was biting his lips; he was pale, and he
said not a word. Annemarie pulled herself together.
She crouched in her seat like a cat, ready to spring,
ready for a life-and-death struggle.

Austin had to decrease his speed; they were approaching a village, and there, at a cross-roads, on the pavement, about a hundred yards before them, was a gendarme.

Austin suddenly applied the brakes. Annemarie saw that his face was distorted with rage. He leaped out of the car and ran quickly towards the gendarme.

"Hullo!" he cried. "Sergeant, come here, quickly!"

At that moment Annemarie stepped on the accelerator. Her other foot released the brakes; she had already slipped in the top gear; with her right hand on the steering-wheel she slid into the driver's seat, and the car shot down the road. It tore out of the village, roaring; in top gear, for Annemarie did not yet understand how to change the gear. By the edge of a wood the car ran on to the grass track beside the road. Annemarie tugged at the emergency brake, but she was not in time to prevent the car colliding with a tree. She jumped out; and the car, since the engine was still in gear, ran on, crossed the road, overturned into the ditch, and burst into flames.

Annemarie fled through the wood. She ran as though for her life. She followed a narrow path which led her to the bank of a canal. There she saw a large motor-barge gliding slowly through the water. She tore off her clothes, and made a bundle of them, tied them on her back, and slipped into the water. She had not far to swim; then she seized the low gunwale of the barge, swung herself on board, crept aft, taking care to remain invisible from the bank, and finally stood in the cockpit, confronting an ancient Dutch bargee, who was so startled by the apparition of this dripping and scantily-clad young lady that his clay pipe fell from his mouth. So soon as Annemarie had recovered breath she tackled the situation.

"Three thousand francs," she said. "Look: here are the notes. They are rather wet, but otherwise they are all right. They are for you, if you get me over the Dutch frontier; guards are after me; I'm supposed to have been smuggling diamonds. Here's a thousand francs on account."

Mevrouw, the bargee's wife, appeared from the cabin in answer to her husband's call. This lady was prompt in action. In the cabin, behind all manner of bales and boxes, was a little door, which might easily be over-looked, and which did not seem to be entirely uncon-nected with smuggling. Behind the door was a sort of cupboard into which a few blankets and pillows were thrown. The bargeman's wife took the fugitive's wet clothes, and gave her many cups of very hot tea. Anne-marie's heart beat as though it would burst; but finally the frontier was crossed, and Mevrouw stood by while her husband received, not only two thousand francs in notes, but also a hearty kiss.

Meanwhile René Austin had not been idle. For some time he and the gendarme were delayed by the burning car; they supposed that the woman was pinned under it. When at last they realized that she had not been burned to death, but had escaped, they notified the *gardes champêtres*, who turned out with their horses and dogs; but in the meantime rain had fallen, and the dogs could find no scent.

In Brussels René Austin produced the missing leaf of Annemarie's notebook, which had not fallen into a pool, but had been carefully preserved in his pocket-book. Both sides of the paper were covered with letters and numerals, which recorded the armaments of two fortresses which the friends had recently visited. The calibres and ranges of all the guns were carefully noted.

At the Hook of Holland Annemarie took the boat for Dover. She had met Matthesius in Amsterdam, and her notes went with him to Berlin. She had altered her appearance. Her hair was done in a different fashion, and she wore glasses. She spent some time in the Isle of Wight, making long motor-boat trips along the English coast, always with her painting gear, and if she was observed she assumed the bearing of an enthusiastic lady artist. And then, suddenly, she was overcome by a dreadful sense of anxiety, just as she had been in the village near Charleville, before Wynanky's death. As then, she was sleeping in a small village inn. She got out of bed in the middle of the night, packed only her most essential belongings in a hand-bag, and crept out on to the landing. Slowly, silently, obeying her inexplicable feeling of dread, she crept down the stairs, and finally stood listening on the ground floor of the house. In the bar-room several men were talking under their breath. She was quite right; they were speaking of her; she was suspected of spying out the coastal defences, and she would shortly be arrested.

On the following day Annemarie Lesser travelled from Dover to Calais by a French steamer. She went on board with a Swiss passport, and she reached Berlin without incident, travelling through Paris, while on all the English boats search was being made for her, as her personal description had been sent out by wireless.

In Berlin Matthesius ascertained that the Belgian and British secret services were working hand in hand, and that they had realized that the spy who had made use of René Austin and the lady artist of the Isle of Wight were one and the same person. On account of her spectacles she had been nicknamed the "lady doctor."

Matthesius took all her passports and threw them into the fire. "I think now you had better go to Meran for a bit, under your own name, and rest, and take things easy. I am afraid, however—but I won't bother you with that now."

Annemarie went to Meran, where she spent her time strolling through the parks and gardens. The events of the last few weeks, her escape on board the Dutch barge, her long walk through the night to Dover, all seemed things of the remote past. She spent much of her time in the company of an Italian jeweller, and it was the first time for years that she had seen much of any man without considering how she might extract some kind of military secret from him.

In the middle of July, 1914, she received instructions from Matthesius to proceed instantly to Italy. A German agent, an ex-officer of the pioneers, who was stationed in Milan, had been instructed by Matthesius to ascertain immediately whether any new earthworks had been constructed in Italy, above all on the coast, and if so, what was their nature and extent. The agent was expected to complete his task within a week or so. He telegraphed to Berlin, in cipher, that he would need some weeks for the task, for he could see no other way of obtaining the information than to travel all over the peninsula. Twenty-four hours after this telegram was received Annemarie Lesser called upon him. On the following day a new advertisement-bureau was opened in the city. That such a business should subscribe to all the newspapers in the country, and above all to the small local journals, did not seem in any way extraordinary. All these newspapers were systematically examined for advertisements in which the military authorities invited tenders for excavations and for work in reinforced concrete. It was then an easy matter, with the help of a good military map, to estimate the nature and extent of the intended fortifications; and in six days the work was done.

CHAPTER SIX

ESPIONAGE IN THE WORLD WAR

THE outbreak of the war upset all theories and prophecies and calculations as to the effect of such an event on the peoples of the countries involved, and their economic life, and even their military operations. At one blow the whole of Europe was thrown into a state of monstrous upheaval; the very face of the world was changed. No one had foreseen, no one could have foreseen, the stupendous nature of the events which now followed in quick succession. In every country men were confronted by situations before which they were at first helpless; the organization of the war behind the fronts was a gradual affair.

The international secret services were instantly and completely disorganized. Secret communication between country and country became impossible. It was only after the war had been proceeding for some weeks that the belligerent Powers realized the necessity of beginning all over again, and of organizing a completely new service.

For England, France and Belgium this necessity was most urgent. Their espionage before the war had been far more active than defensive; in particular, they had applied themselves to obtaining details of the German frontier defences, in order to determine the route to be followed by their own troops on German territory. Above all, they had striven to ascertain the German plans of mobilization, in order to discover any strategic or tactical weaknesses the knowledge of which would enable them to hinder the German advance, so that their own troops might the sooner achieve a decisive success and penetrate into enemy territory.

The stupendous success of the German Army in the first weeks of the war on the Western front resulted in the automatic scrapping of all their measures. The greater part of the labours of the British and French secret services, which had worked with such ample means, such remarkable skill, and such admirable energy, had been undertaken in vain. The information which they had procured was useless, for France was desperately defending her own territory, and England had to come to her assistance. For the time being no attack on the German coastal defences could be contemplated. From the very first the military situation fluctuated from hour to hour; the area of hostilities itself was constantly changing. In short, as has been said, all calculations were completely upset, and there was nothing for it but to begin all over again. At first the Allies confined themselves to attacking the German secret service, which, by the very nature of things, since the Germans were fighting in France, was still of considerable value. The Germans had in Antwerp an extraordinarily skilful and efficient agent, whose reports, before the war, referred more particularly to the co-operation of the British, French and Belgian military authorities. At the very outset of the war the Belgians arrested this man and shot him. His existence, and the fact that he was a spy, had been revealed to them by the English Intelligence Service.

All things considered, the English struck the German Intelligence Service the hardest blow during the early days of the war. We know to-day that even before the war the authorities had full particulars of the principal German spies in England, though we do not know who betrayed these people. Until the outbreak of the war these agents were left absolutely undisturbed, so that they must have believed themselves to be perfectly secure; but within a few hours of the outbreak of the war they were seized and imprisoned. Some twenty persons were thus arrested. This was a serious matter for German espionage, since the news from England was, of course, peculiarly important. A short time after the outbreak of the war a very important member of the German Intelligence Service was arrested: the naval officer Karl Hans Lody. He was shot in the Tower; compelling the respect of all who came into contact with him by his courageous bearing. He died the death of a hero for his Fatherland.

Russia, having built up a system of espionage on a basis of unprecedented breadth, was the only belligerent Power to escape the prevailing confusion in respect of the organization of espionage. In the first place, the Russian armies had actually invaded German soil, and, as was proved by the Redl case, their espionage in

Austria was so well organized that it was able to secure information which was likely to be, and actually was, of the greatest value in the event of war. But in respect of the military secrets of Germany they had not ascertained anything very essential. This comparative lack of success was due to the nature of the organization of their espionage in Germany.

While the German authorities were racking their brains over the organization of German espionage in the enemy countries, the amateur counter-espionage of the German people began to assume the most alarming forms. The chief of the German Intelligence Service, Colonel Nikolai, says in his book *Geheime Mächte*:

"The populace was hearing of these things from official sources for the first time. The consequence was a frantic terror of spies throughout the country, which led to ridiculous but also very serious phenomena. The most insane rumours spread like wildfire in times of intense national excitement. In particular, the rumour that motor-cars were carrying gold for the purposes of the enemy secret services had disastrous results. Every car was held up, and the occupants were fired on if they attempted to proceed. Highly placed officials travelling in the service of the State lost their lives in this manner. Within a few days a state of affairs had come about which imperilled the completion of the mobilization."

There is an official document which gives a by no means exaggerated picture of the conditions then prevailing in Germany. It is an official order which the chief of the Stuttgart police, Police-Director Bittinger, issued to the officers and men under his command. It runs as follows:

"To the police of Stuttgart: The inhabitants are beginning to go crazy; the streets are full of old women of both sexes, who are devoting themselves to the most deplorable activities. Each of them sees in his neighbour a French or Russian spy, and thinks it his duty to break his head, and that of the policeman who takes his part, or at the very least to collect a great mob and deliver him to the police. Clouds are seen as aeroplanes, stars as dirigibles, and bicycle lamps as bombs; telephone and telegraph wires are supposed to have been cut in the centre of Stuttgart; it is said that bridges have been blown up, and spies shot by the authorities, and that the water-supply has been poisoned. It is impossible to foresee what form this sort of thing will assume if things should really go badly with us. As a matter of fact, up to the present nothing whatever suspicious has occurred. Nevertheless, one might believe oneself in a madhouse; whereas everyone, if he is not a coward or a dangerous idler, ought to be doing his duty; the times are serious enough. Constables, continue to keep cool; be as you have been hitherto, men, and not women; do not allow yourselves to be intimidated; and keep your eyes open, as is your duty. —POLICE-DIRECTOR BITTINGER."

One of the most respectable of German newspapers, a Frankfort journal, went so far as to publish the following paragraph (18th September, 1914):

"In Walbech, on the 2nd August, 1914, eighty French officers in German uniform were arrested, who had dashed across the German frontier in twelve motor-cars. In Berlin numbers of secret agents were arrested; and in Unter den Linden two Russian women spies, disguised as deaconesses, were apprehended."

That this psychosis ever existed was the fault of a system which in time of peace scrupulously kept from the public all knowledge of such cases of espionage as did occur in Germany. Apparently the authorities were afraid that the prestige of the Army might suffer if they admitted that foreign spies had obtained valuable information. Apart from the initiated, no German knew anything about the real nature and methods of espionage, and this ignorance had grievous results. While rumours of spies in deaconesses' robes were flying about, the people had no knowledge of the real nature of espionage, and were consequently unable effectively to co-operate in preventing and detecting it.

Meanwhile, in all the belligerent countries the intelligence services had attained unprecedented dimensions; they had been reorganized and enormously expanded. The neutral countries were overrun with the intelligence agents of the belligerent Powers; the bureaux which already existed were enlarged and extended. The number of their agents was increased a hundredfold. All espionage during the war was essentially of the following character: Innumerable agents provided with neutral passes travelled all over Europe. They were attracted to the service merely by the money which they could earn. It sounds grotesque, but it has been abundantly proved that bureaux were presently established—principally in Holland—which sold information much as a news agency sells news. It was quite indifferent to them to whom they sold it; the important thing was that it should fetch the best possible price. The espionage of the Great War, since innumerable spies were sent out by all countries and in all directions, reduced itself to nothing more than a problem in arithmetic which had to be solved in the central bureaux. All that could be done was to determine, by arithmetical calculation, which items of information were probably reliable and which were not. It was necessary also to estimate whether it was worth while, in a strategical sense, to take counter-measures against such measures of the enemy's as had apparently been ascertained. The important thing, of course, was to be able to tell genuine information from false, and important from unimportant. Owing to the enormous number of agents who were recruited from all sides during the war, and the even greater number who offered their services for the reasons already stated, it was impossible to form any opinion of the credibility of individual spies. This was quickly realized by all the belligerent Powers. Consequently, over and above this wholesale espionage of all against all there was a certain amount of individual espionage. By this I mean the dispatch of specially qualified and reliable persons, who, from the nature of the case, were mostly officers. Such men were given a free hand, or at most were furnished with very general directions.

These spies, as events proved, were always the most successful; they were trustworthy and financially disinterested, and they were inspired by patriotism or soldierly ambition. In addition to such men adventurers of every nationality played a part in the work of espionage which lifted them above the ruck of the ordinary agents; they were spies of greater importance, because they were, for the most part, of greater intelligence. The most notorious representative of this type of spy was the dancer, Mata Hari. As for the wholesale kind of espionage, things eventually came to such a pass that the intelligence bureaux of the different countries had finally to require their agents to furnish proof of the accuracy of their statements. In all the intelligence bureaux of the belligerent countries an enormous number of such "proofs" were accumulated. It may be said at once that they were mostly forged. Some agents brought what were apparently the originals of important army orders which they professed to have acquired in some fantastic manner. Many of these documents were accepted as genuine, and paid for; others were immediately recognized as forgeries; all that the forger cared about was the money he hoped to receive for the document. The author heard one

very characteristic story from the lips of a man who
was at the head of the intelligence service in a country
which was at first neutral, but which subsequently entered the war against Germany.

In this country, shortly after it entered into the war,
a very large ammunition depot was blown up. Before
the day was over no less than eight persons had called
upon my informant, each of whom laid claim to a very
large reward, because it was he, and he alone, who had
blown up the ammunition depot!

The technical side of wholesale espionage need not
be further particularized. The description of a calling
whose representatives are one and all morally inferior
cannot be especially interesting. But the fates of the
great military spies who are actuated by love of their
native country, and the fates of the great adventurers
in espionage—these are worth recording.

CHAPTER SEVEN

THE "LADY DOCTOR" IN THE WAR

ANNEMARIE LESSER had intended to spend a few weeks in Capri, but in Rome she received the first warning of the threatening storm: the European war was imminent. Annemarie hurried from Rome to Milan in a high-powered car; there, with the help of the permanent German agents, she obtained a French passport in a false name; and then the storm broke; the war seemed now inevitable. Annemarie hurried on to Ventimiglia, in the same car, which she then sent back; and presently a French nursing-sister was making her way to Paris.

In Paris, at the end of July, she broke in upon Monsieur Pissard, the permanent agent.

She found a man pale with terror, and trembling as he sat in his chair. He gazed in surprise at the intruder. Annemarie said, quietly:

"Don't look at me like that. One and four, G and W."

Then Pissard sprang to his feet, with a look of relief. "The 'lady doctor'! You have ventured to come to Paris?"

In frantic haste Pissard laid his papers before the German spy. Outside his windows the mob, raving with bellicose enthusiasm, was singing the Marseillaise; while the individual voices were shouting: "À Berlin, à Berlin!" Pissard had not been idle during these stirring days; by constantly haunting the railway stations and getting into conversation with the mobilized soldiers he had ascertained the details of the French advance. Within an hour the "lady doctor" had heard all Pissard's explanations, and had copied all his information on very thin paper, which she then concealed upon her person.

With the assistance of Pissard, who always had the necessary materials at hand, she prepared herself a new passport. She was now the daughter of a Belgian officer, and she drew up a document to the effect that in the event of war she was at once to be attached, as a Belgian nurse, to a Belgian field hospital.

But when she sought a means of proceeding at once to Belgium she encountered the most appalling difficulties. She ventured everything; she walked into the lion's den, into the transport department of the garrison of Paris, where her seductive charm, and her way of smiling from under drooping eyelashes, were too much for the transport officer; and she succeeded in securing a seat in the "courier" car which was to take certain officers of the French General Staff, dressed in civilian clothing, from Paris to Brussels. The car passed through Compiègne, St. Quentin, Maubeuge and Charleroi, and the trained eyes of the "lady doctor" were at once able to detect the critical points of the French advance, and to note its weak points. She learned much from her conversation with the French staff officers, and amongst other things the enormously important fact, which hitherto the German General Staff had only suspected, that in case of war the Belgian Army would fight side by side with the French.

When the car reached Brussels Annemarie was unable at once to get away from the French officers. As a matter of fact, they insisted on accompanying her to the Belgian General Staff, where she was present during a conversation between the Belgian officers and the *sous-chef* of the French General Staff. She—as an enthusiastic Belgian patriot—learned that the chief of the Belgian General Staff, General de Ryckel, foresaw an offensive war against Germany. She learned further that so soon as the first shot was fired six divisions of British infantry and eight brigades of cavalry—a total strength of a hundred and sixty thousand men—would be landed at Antwerp.

Annemarie Lesser listened to this conversation with mixed feelings. On the one hand, she knew that this information was of enormous importance to the German Army, if only she could reach Berlin in time to deliver it. On the other hand, she was perfectly well aware that she was in terrible danger of being unmasked if it should occur to General de Ryckel to look a little more closely into her personal references. Accordingly she made her escape at the earliest possible moment; she had to make various purchases: but she was unable to avoid an appointment with one of the French officers, a staff major, for that evening, at the

Palace Hotel; an appointment which she was the less
able to avoid inasmuch as this officer was already head
over ears in love with her.

As she stood on the pavement outside the headquarters of the General Staff she made up her mind that she
would not keep this appointment.   But by the evening
her adventurous spirit had conquered her prudence. She
risked her life in order to learn yet more, and before
she had been an hour in the company of her host, in
the dining-room of the Palace Hotel, she had ascertained the Belgian plan of advance.   She learned that
the military governor of the Belgian provinces had been
instructed that he was not to regard the movements
of French troops on Belgian territory as a violation of
neutrality.   The Belgian Army would be drawn up on
either side of the Gete in the area Hannut—St. Trond
—Tirlemont—Hamme—Mille.   She learned all the
details of this advance, and by midnight she had ascertained that the fortress of Liège had been fully manned.
And above all, she was acquainted with the technical
condition of the works.   The forts were modern and
supposed to be proof against direct hits, but the earthworks in the intervals of the forts had not undergone
any very recent improvements, and the country in front
of the forts, which was traversed by deep ravines, was
entirely out of the line of direct fire.   There were no
outlying subterranean forts in these valleys.   The
fortress itself was to be occupied immediately by two
divisions, while the 3rd and the 4th Belgian divisions
would cover the advance of these troops to Liège. When

Annemarie had learned these things she knew that she could waste no more time in the society of her admirer.

She complained of feeling suddenly unwell; and the thought of her "father," the Belgian officer, filled her with anxiety. She succeeded in taking her leave of the officer without arousing his resentment, and by means of her passport and her forged references she was able to secure a seat in the Liège express—the very train in which the officers of the Belgian General Staff were hastening to the fortress.

Matthesius was in Berlin. For days he had not left his room. Bundles of telegrams from all parts of the world were accumulating on his desk. There were two telephones in the room; they were not silent for a moment. Orderly officers in uniform were passing in and out.

But in the midst of his uninterrupted labours there was one constant thought at the back of his mind: where is Annemarie Lesser? A cipher telegram had told him that she was entering France by way of Ventimiglia. Either she has been arrested and shot, he told himself, or she is on her way here, and with information of extraordinary importance. He awaited her return, and her information, with the greatest anxiety, now that all communication with Paris and Brussels was interrupted; the threat of immediate war had made it impossible for his agents to use the telegraph.

On the night of the 3rd August an outpost of the

German frontier forces, on the frontier between Belgium and Germany, challenged a woman on the Nasproue-Eupen road. She was dressed like a peasant, with a shawl over her head, and thick woollen stockings, but the soldier noticed that she was wearing thin and very well-made shoes. This woman, who by some unknown means had crossed the frontier, asked to be taken at once to the officer in command. This was in the middle of the night. The lieutenant in command of the platoon was wakened. He decided that this woman was a highly suspicious person. A midwife was fetched, and no one paid any attention to the woman's angry protests that she must at once see an officer of the General Staff. The search conducted by the midwife revealed innumerable closely-written sheets of paper and a Belgian pass. "You blockhead!" cried the woman to the lieutenant. "Of course I am a spy—but a German spy! If you can't take me immediately to an officer of the General Staff, do at least telegraph to Berlin, to the Great General Staff, telling them that you have just arrested agent one and four, G and W!"

The woman was left in the custody of the midwife and two sentries. The lieutenant waked his captain; an urgent service telegram was sent to Berlin, and an hour later a motor-car drove into the little village, and in the car was an officer of the General Staff. Never in his life had anyone roared at the lieutenant as the staff officer roared at him now. Presently the momentous information was being telephoned, word for word, to Matthesius in Berlin. Matthesius took it down and put it into shape, and a few hours later the message was on its way back to the troops at the front, in the form of instructions and orders.

On the afternoon of August 4th General von Emmich received permission to march into Belgium, together with the order to attempt an assault on Liège, since in the light of "the information of agents" there was a good prospect of success.

The fortress of Liège fell on the 6th of August.

During the first weeks of the war Matthesius removed to another address. His little office in Bülowstrasse had become inadequate; and he was allotted a whole house, a fine old building in Königgrätzer Strasse. Before long the house was busy as a beehive, and the rooms of the first and second floors were full of officers in uniform or mufti. Here all the threads of the secret service ran together; and from this centre the information received, after it had been collated and scrutinized and sifted, was forwarded to the military authorities. In the third storey of the house—in every sense over all the rest—Matthesius himself sat working almost night and day, and in the same room Annemarie Lesser had her desk.

The activities of this establishment, and especially those of the third floor, were very like those of the editorial offices of a great newspaper. There were, of course, certain differences. No general news was received; but innumerable persons flocked thither who were lured by the scent of money, and who offered to act as spies in enemy countries, and behind the fronts of the hostile armies. These people had applied in the first place to the military authorities, and if the competent officer was convinced that a man was really fitted for the service he was given an appointment with Matthesius, and only when he had actually delivered information which proved to be accurate was he directed to the bureau installed in the old house in Königgrätzer Strasse. But only the really eminent spies, only the most successful and reliable, ever found their way to the room on the third floor.

It was not long before Matthesius began to feel the effects of overwork. His clothes flapped on his emaciated limbs; his face was more haggard than ever; his hands fidgeted incessantly with his pencils and compasses. The "lady doctor" was promoted. In the place of the overworked Matthesius, it was she who now interviewed those who applied for employment as spies; she had a wonderful way of dealing with these difficult people; she soon divided the tares from the wheat, and on two occasions she was able to unmask an enemy spy. In each case the spy was a French officer who had entered Germany by way of Switzerland in order to offer his services to the German Intelligence Service, and in that way to trace out the network of German agents. Annemarie had the gift of estimating at sight the probability of each item of information, and its positive or negative value. With the exception of a short visit to England, where most of the German agents had been betrayed and arrested on the outbreak of the war, so that it became necessary to establish fresh connections, she remained in Berlin until the beginning of 1916, until the German attack upon Verdun was secretly decided upon.

At this moment, when it was of the greatest importance to Germany that the intelligence service in France should operate promptly and reliably, all communications with that country suddenly broke down.

Most of the information relating to France had been supplied by Pissard, a French citizen, who was always prompt and accurate. At intervals of a few days secret messengers, travelling always by different routes, foregathered with him in Paris, immediately afterwards proceeding to a neutral country. Monsieur Pissard's firm, Meunier & Co., had now a branch office in Switzerland, and their confidential clerk came to Paris every week to consult with him. Moreover, Pissard had agents in many of the small French towns, who pushed the sale of Messieurs Meunier's pneumatic tyres and ball-bearings, and to whom he had to pay periodical visits.

In the critical days before the intended attack on Verdun this source of information suddenly and unexpectedly failed. Pissard was not to be found; his office was closed, and no one knew what had become of him.

Annemarie Lesser decided at once to go to Paris, in order to learn what had happened. There was no time to be lost; nevertheless, she omitted no precautions. She went from Holland to England and from England to Bordeaux, so that no one should suspect her purpose. She too found the office of Meunier & Co. closed; but a woman of her courage and intelligence was not to be baulked by a locked door. She succeeded in entering the office, and in ascertaining what had happened to the agent.

Monsieur Pissard had been called up. But on the day on which he was to have joined his regiment his overwrought nerves had failed him, and the man who had hitherto been a richly rewarded spy of the enemy had shot himself through the head.

Annemarie Lesser did not hesitate. Unshaken by the tragic end of the German agent, she took steps to replace him.

In Berlin a man by the name of Constantine Coudoyanis had sought her out, and had offered his services as a German spy in France. He was a Greek subject, and was the Paris representative of firms which exported Mediterranean fruits. Annemarie now called on Coudoyanis at his house in Paris. Coudoyanis, who had formerly been an officer in the Greek Army, but was for some reason or other dismissed the service, now acquired the firm of Meunier & Co. from the heirs, two elderly spinsters from Marseilles; and he was able to do this with safety, since hitherto neither the firm nor its late agent had been regarded with the slightest suspicion.

Annemarie remained for a time in France, and she did something of which Coudoyanis had no knowledge. During the course of a Sunday excursion she came across a *sous-officier* who was attached to the counter-espionage department of the French General Staff. In a couple of days this man had fallen a victim to the charms of the beautiful spy. From him Annemarie learned many things worth knowing; and Matthesius, in Berlin, breathed freely again, for information was once more arriving; information of a reliable nature and of inestimable importance. And now Annemarie threw all that she possessed into the scale. The *sous-officier* was under the impression that she had been a professional hanger-on of the cafés and cabarets of Montmartre and the great boulevards, and was quite convinced that it was owing to his good influence that the girl was on the way to becoming a good, respectable *bourgeoise*. One day they went for a walk together, and he asked her to marry him. Annemarie accepted his proposal, provided her parents approved. They were living in a little town by the Spanish frontier. Annemarie travelled south to see them.

As a matter of fact, she had an interview that very evening with a German officer whom the Intelligence Service had sent to Paris. This man knew nothing of the existence of Constantine Coudoyanis, and the Greek knew nothing of the German officer, who had been sent to obtain news of importance to the German High Command.

She then went as far from Paris as she could without exciting suspicion. At Fontainebleau she met an agent who was sent to her by Matthesius, gave him all the information in her possession, and returned to Paris, which she reached during the afternoon.

She had often met her lover, the *sous-officier*, out-

side his office. She used to wait in the street until he
appeared; and he was almost always punctual. But
this evening she had to wait a long while. When her
friend finally appeared he was overjoyed to hear the
message which Annemarie had brought from her "parents." They approved of the marriage; nevertheless
he was nervous and excited.

"But what is it, my dear—what's the matter with
you?"

"Well, you see, this has been a cheerful sort of day!
Sacré nom de Dieu! Two of our agents have announced that they have seen someone in this country
who is on our list of German spies. It's a woman; and
if she is really running about the country it's no joke
at all, for this is a most capable person."

"A woman?" asked Annemarie Lesser. "What's her
name?"

"That we don't know; we've only got a very bad
photograph of her; it was taken in Brussels, a long
time ago; she is with some Belgian officers. We know
only her nickname—the 'lady doctor.' But that's
enough of her; let us talk of ourselves!"

On the following day all the official publications contained the information that a German woman spy was
travelling about the country. Her appearance was ap-
proximately so and so; and half a million francs would
be paid for her apprehension. That evening Annemarie requested Coudoyanis to send his fiancée—a
pretty young dancer—to Bordeaux. According to a
theatrical journal, a dancer of her type was wanted in

one of the cabarets of that city. They would then have someone in Bordeaux who could keep a record of incoming vessels, and learn much else of importance. Coudoyanis objected strongly, but Annemarie was adamant, and the Greek was not the man to withstand her. That very evening he initiated his fiancée; that very evening the dancer learned the nature of her lover's activities. She was to proceed to Bordeaux in four days' time. She was engaged, without delay, by telegraph, as she was told to offer her services for a very small salary.

On the following evening Annemarie had once more to wait a long while before her lover appeared. Once more, when he did appear, he was nervous and excited.

"Someone came to see us to-day," he said, "who wants to deliver the 'lady doctor' to the firing squad. But he is asking for an advance of a hundred thousand francs. He's a Greek, Coudoyanis by name. We are having him watched at this moment, although he doesn't suspect it, and to-morrow morning he will call again. We shall give him the hundred thousand francs, and to-morrow night he will betray the spy to us. He says that he saw her once in Berlin before the war, and now he has recognized her in Paris."

"Will it be good for you if they catch her? Will you be promoted?" asked Annemarie Lesser, nestling fondly against him.

That night "the lady doctor" made an appointment to meet Coudoyanis in a café. When he was on the way to keep the appointment he was overtaken by a

taxicab in which sat Annemarie Lesser. She quickly
gave him an envelope, and told him that at seven o'clock
the following morning a German agent would meet him
in a small tavern on the outskirts of Paris, and would
pay him fifty thousand francs as a special remuneration. After a short conversation Annemarie left the
taxi. She noticed that someone was following her at a
run, but this she had expected, and she easily evaded
her pursuer.

That night the French counter-espionage bureau received a startling piece of information. It was contained
in a typewritten letter, delivered by express post. The
letter stated that Constantine Coudoyanis was a German spy. It was a good French patriot who accused
him; he would not give his name, lest the Germans
should seek to revenge themselves on him; but if the
authorities did not believe him, let them send the following morning, at seven o'clock, to such and such a
tavern. There they would find Coudoyanis, and he
would have upon him a letter directed to a German
agent with whom he had an appointment, and which
would contain important military information. To make
even more certain, they had better that very night arrest and question his fiancée, a dancer, who was to be
found at such and such an address. This dancer knew
that Coudoyanis was a German spy; he had even intended to send her to Bordeaux, so that she might obtain
information for him.

Coudoyanis was arrested next morning in the tavern
which had been indicated. The letter to the German

agent was found on him. His fiancée, the dancer, confessed to everything, and Constantine Coudoyanis refused to the day of his death to make any admissions as to his activities, or the person for whom he had worked. A few days after his arrest he was sentenced to death, and the night of his execution, when the drum was already summoning the firing-party, he told the captain of engineers who was then in his cell:

"It may perhaps be of advantage to you to know, Monsieur, that it is a woman who has brought me to my death."

Then he was silent. Only when he heard the words of command which told him that the firing-party had already taken up their position did he speak again.

"She was a wonderfully beautiful woman. She was extremely clever, and amazingly energetic. She had such an influence over me that I could not resist her. She mastered everyone who came into contact with her; even officers of the highest rank. She was actuated not by avarice, but by passion and inclination. I hope, Monsieur le Capitaine, that you will never meet such a woman."

At the very moment when the Greek met his death Annemarie Lesser was entering Berlin.

In June, 1917, all the belligerent countries began the wholesale recruiting of men for the final struggle, which, after all, must come sooner or later. Had the men who had attained military age during the past year already been enlisted? To what arms of the service had they been allotted, and above all, how soon would

145

they be sufficiently trained to take the field? These were questions which neither Matthesius nor Annemarie Lesser was for the moment in a position to answer, though the military authorities were constantly pressing them for information. They would have to wait a few weeks until they could be sure that the available recruits had been called up; then they could angle for information in the garrisons of the enemy countries.

A day before the instructions to this effect were to be forwarded to the chief agent in Paris something quite unforeseen occurred. A courier arrived from Switzerland bringing terrible news from Paris. It had been ascertained that the French counter-espionage bureau had for some weeks had a list in its possession which contained the personal description of the most important of the German agents then working in the larger French cities. A man who had been employed since the days of Pissard had been guilty of some imprudence; he had been arrested and unmasked as a German spy. The authorities had promised him not only his life, but his freedom and a large sum of money if he would betray his colleagues. He had not hesitated to save his life at their expense.

The chief agent in Paris, a German officer, who had been inducted into his duties by Annemarie Lesser while Coudoyanis was still alive, announced that it was not known how many agents the man had betrayed; he could not even say how much the detected spy knew about the German agents in France and their methods of procedure. One thing, however, was certain: the chief agent himself had been betrayed, and he stated that the letter which he was now dispatching, and in which he announced this terrible news, was probably the last which he would be able to get out of the country. But in spite of everything he would remain at his post, and regard himself as an officer at the front.

When Annemarie Lesser had decoded this message she laid it in silence before Matthesius. They were both overwhelmed by the news. Apparently the French intended to allow the agents to continue at work undisturbed for a time, while they quietly kept them under observation, until they were able to seize them all simultaneously and send them before the firing-squad. And they would surely do this at some moment when it was particularly important for them to conceal, and for the Germans to ascertain, the measures which were being taken behind the front.

If this plan was successful the German High Command would find itself without information at the very moment when the French were planning a decisive blow. When this was clear to both the colleagues Annemarie Lesser declared: "I shall go to Paris."

During the whole time of their work together this was the only occasion on which Matthesius earnestly sought to dissuade her from a perilous undertaking.

She required three days to make her preparations for her dangerous venture. For three days Matthesius never saw her. And when she did appear he was furious.

"How did you get into this room? What do you want here? Who are you?"

It was some time before even his experienced eyes could recognize his colleague. Before him stood a girl with Titian-red hair, a muddy complexion, a slovenly dress, down-trodden shoes, darned stockings, puffy features, and a stupid expression.

Some days later this girl was in Paris, applying to the employment-agencies for a place as domestic servant. She was then wearing a still clean but rather tattered blue cloak and an impossible straw hat with red ribbons. She came from Normandy. She had been in service in Toulon, but her employers, who were English, had discharged her in Paris, as they were returning to England. She showed her references; she was "diligent, willing and honest." In almost every agency she was offered employment, but she could not make up her mind; she wandered about the streets and gazed at the monuments and public buildings, carrying her possessions in a cardboard box, and asking various concièrges if they could tell her of anyone who wanted a servant.

In several cases they were able to do so, but she always decided that she would have to think things over. One evening she spoke to the concièrge of a large house in the Rue François: No. 3. The ground floor was apparently unoccupied; on the first floor were offices, and the rest of the house consisted of an *hôtel garni*.

Just about this time the German agents in France received a warning to escape as quickly as possible to neutral countries. The chief agent and his three sub-ordinates escaped over the Spanish frontier; the rest were one and all arrested as they were boarding their trains.

A dozen men of different nationalities, fearless of death, set out from Berlin and entered France by various routes, in order to replace the dispersed or arrested agents.

No. 3 Rue François was no ordinary house. Both the offices and the furnished apartments were recent innovations. In short, this old and somewhat gloomy exterior now sheltered the civil bureau of the central office for counter-espionage in France. In the offices upstairs were French officers in civilian dress; the furnished apartments harboured the agents who arrived in Paris at all hours of the day and night, by all imaginable routes, and from all quarters of the Continent. In the offices the lights were burning day and night, and the common sitting-rooms of the *hôtel garni* were always full of men and women, coming and going, talking and listening. Annemarie Lesser would never have ventured into this building if she had had reason to fear that her late fiancé, the *sous-officier* of the military branch of the counter-espionage department, might still be at his post, for the military branch worked in close co-operation with the bureau in the Rue François; but she knew that he had rejoined his regiment some considerable time before her return to Paris.

The concièrge of the house had referred Annemarie to the manageress of the *hôtel garni* upstairs. Here the reputed Norman, who gave the manageress the impression of being an incredibly honest and fantastically stupid young person, was engaged for an infinitesimal wage; but she received full board, and a bed in a room which she shared with three other girls. Her duties consisted in scrubbing the floors and stairs and washing dishes. She worked in this house for a fortnight. She washed the staircases; she swept out the faded and indescribably grimy sitting-rooms; she washed up the plates and dishes; and in the midst of her heavy and unaccustomed labours she had only one source of relief; a terribly dangerous solace, which was one day to prove disastrous.

In the evening, after a day of running up and down the stairs, while the scum of the rabble of international agents pinched her calves as she passed them—after stilling her hunger as best she could with the bad and scanty meals provided—she sought relief in an injection of morphia. It was while she was in this house that she began to need more than one injection daily.

At the end of a fortnight she began to draw the threads together. At night, from one o'clock, when the officers had left the building, to the early hours of the morning, there were only two non-commissioned officers in the offices. The rooms had to be swept and dusted in the presence of the two soldiers. The duty of cleaning out the rooms in the morning fell upon the four girls in rotation, and it soon emerged, in Annemarie's conversations with her fellow-servants, that she was the poorest of the four. The night work was a burden to these girls, who had to be up again by seven o'clock or earlier, and the three were well content to find that the fourth, in return for a trifling payment, was ready to undertake the night work permanently. Before long the girl from Normandy was on friendly terms with one of the non-commissioned officers. During the hours of his night duty she often sat with him, and when all was quiet in the offices he told her of his little farm, which lay in the area occupied by the German troops, and of his wife and daughter, from whom he heard only rarely and at irregular intervals.

On the Sunday of the fourth week of her presence in the house this man was alone on duty. Sunday was the one day in the week on which only one of the *sous-officiers* was on night duty in the offices.

That night the soldier gazed with amazement at the girl from Normandy. Where had his eyes been? This girl was really extremely pretty! Her eyes, which at other times had been so dull and apathetic, were actually sparkling with merriment, and she was teasing and provoking him. Presently, as he was sitting at a table, she came behind him and playfully covered his eyes. Laughing, the soldier felt for her wrists: and suddenly a cloth fell over his eyes, and he felt something moist and repellently sweet against his nose and mouth; his blood hummed in his brain, and then he knew no more. That night a girl in a blue cloak left the house in the Rue François; a girl much younger and prettier than the servant-maid from Normandy.

In the morning the telegraph was busy; messages

were flying from the house in the Rue François to all the frontier stations, and all the military frontier guards whose duty it was to watch the trains. All day the Morse keys were ticking, for a terrible thing had happened. A *sous-officier* in the civil bureau of the counter-espionage department had been made insensible by means of an anæsthetic. All documents, lists and papers relating to the French agents, not only in Germany, but also in the neutral countries, had been stolen, and the thief was apparently a woman who had been employed in the building as a maidservant.

The telegrams were sent in vain. They had the result, indeed, that all women who were attempting to cross the frontier were sharply questioned as to their identity, while their papers and their luggage were subjected to a searching examination; but these measures were of no avail. History—the history of espionage—tells of an evening when a woman fled from France into Switzerland, crossing the frontier by a secret path. And within five hundred yards of the Swiss frontier three dead men were subsequently found—two frontier guards and a soldier—and each of the men had a revolver bullet in his heart.

But in Germany the authorities were preparing to strike a great and effective blow against the secret service of the enemy.

Annemarie Lesser was once more working in Berlin. The events of the last few years had left their trace upon her. She had accustomed herself to a strange way of living. For days at a time she saw no human face. Matthesius himself could not always entice her from her quiet room on the third floor of the house in the Königgrätzer Strasse. Even the most important news did not reach her at once if she had shut herself in for the day.

But when the darkness came, when the lamps were lit in the third storey, Annemarie made her appearance. She crept along the thickly carpeted corridors and sat silently at her desk. Her eyes glittered and her cheeks glowed; morphia and cocaine were beginning to have their effect; at night her brain worked accurately, swiftly, and with almost uncanny insight. She ate hardly anything in these days; a few slices of toast and caviare, washed down with a heavy burgundy, constituted, for days at a time, her sole nourishment. It was as much as Matthesius could do to persuade her now and again to add a few lightly boiled eggs to her menu. It was with consternation that he watched the havoc which her unnatural manner of life was working upon this still beautiful woman.

In this condition she interviewed, during the night, the agents who had arrived in Berlin during the day, receiving their reports, comparing, sketching and calculating, devoting herself indefatigably to her difficult and responsible work.

On the great chess-board of the world war the pieces were now disposed for the final struggle. The spring offensive of the year 1918 had broken through the Western front. What would come next? This depended to a very great extent on the spirit prevailing in the French Army. And it was important also to know where the French intended to parry the blow which they would receive, and what forces were still at their disposal. Where would they strike the counter-blow?

To discover this was a task of infinite difficulty. At the threatened points, wherever the German troops had broken through the enemy lines, the French troops had been so far withdrawn that only the outposts of the armies were in occasional contact. But the outposts of the enemy were exceptionally strong; the operations of the troops behind the front were completely screened; the German High Command was entirely ignorant of the enemy's intentions. This ignorance was a very serious matter, as if the enemy were to deliver a great offensive on some particular sector, extensive movements of troops would be necessary in order successfully to oppose this offensive, and this movement would involve a loss of time.

The new German agents in France were by no means asleep, but information was coming in only from individual sectors, and it was impossible to obtain a clear conception of the situation as a whole.

It was then that the "lady doctor" prepared for her last great *coup*. To begin with, she proceeded to Spain. Whether the rumour was correct which asserted that she went thither on a submarine is uncertain, and to-day it can hardly be confirmed or denied. How she travelled we do not really know, and she herself is no longer capable of giving an account of her journey.

One thing, however, we do know: that late in the spring of 1918 she appeared in Barcelona. She was then wearing the rather conspicuous costume of a South American woman; she was the wife of a planter from one of the states of Spanish South America, who had placed herself at the disposal of the Spanish officials of the Red Cross, and had brought with her large sums of money from her native plantations, which were to be applied to alleviating the sufferings of the wounded.

Her activities were effective and comprehensive. Her energy and enthusiasm persuaded a few Spanish ladies to apply for a permit which would enable a Spanish delegation of the Red Cross to visit the field-hospitals of the French Army. This delegation was to consist only of women. Diplomatic relations were exploited, representations were forwarded, and after a considerable delay the Spanish ladies received the necessary permission.

Not one of the seven women who accompanied Anne-marie Lesser on this journey had the faintest suspicion of the actual purposes of the wealthy and distinguished, if somewhat *exaltée*, Spanish American.

A transport column was organized. Clothing and provisions, necessaries and luxuries were packed into two large motor-vans, two powerful passenger-cars were secured, and the party set out on their journey.

Their route lay along the Western front. From field-hospital to field-hospital, from *étape* to *étape*, the party of benevolent Spanish ladies proceeded on its way, chivalrously entertained and escorted by the

French officers. From south to north they went, and back from north to south, always a few thousand yards behind the most advanced field-hospitals. One evening in mid-August, on the homeward journey, they came to a small field-hospital on the Marne which the officers and nursing sisters had christened "St. Marie de Notre Cœur."

To this hospital, during the course of the day, a great number of wounded had been brought, both officers and men, the victims of a sudden attack on the part of the Germans. The hospital was full to overflowing. When the Spanish ladies asked the surgeon-major in command what they could do for the wounded, they received the laconic reply: "Give a hand!" The ladies needed no persuasion; their dust-cloaks were cast aside and were replaced by white hospital overalls, and the staff of the hospital received a sudden but most welcome reinforcement.

Annemarie Lesser was allotted to the head sister; she was instructed to see that the wounded who came from the operating-table or the dressing-post were put to bed in a large tent. More than a hundred cots were ready to receive the sufferers.

From the operating-theatre the bearers brought her two officers. One was a captain of the French General Staff; while travelling behind the front in a motor-car he had received a shrapnel bullet in the shoulder. The other was a Belgian sapper officer, who had been attached, as liaison officer, to a French infantry regiment, and who had received a rifle-bullet in the leg. The stretcher-bearers brought the two officers into the tent; the head sister attended to the French captain, and Annemarie Lesser helped the bearers to get the Belgian lieutenant to bed. She settled the pillows under his head, and the officer, fully conscious despite his wound, and in full possession of his faculties, begged for a cigarette; there were some in the pocket of his tunic. As Annemarie was bending over him to give him a light the Belgian officer started. The colour fled from his face; he stared at his nurse, struck aside the hand that was holding the match, and cried:

"Orderly! Comrades! Quick, this woman is a German spy!"

The French staff captain, despite the agony of his wound, answered him:

"Who is? Where is the spy?"

The Belgian pointed to Annemarie Lesser.

"Don't talk such nonsense!" she cried. "I am a member of the Red Cross; I have come here from South America!" She spoke with a good-natured smile, and added: "You are seeing ghosts, my dear man!" But her heart sank within her. She knew who the Belgian officer was who had recognized her. He was René Austin, with whom she had flirted in Brussels, who had already once unmasked her, and from whom she had escaped by boarding a Dutch motor-barge.

The Belgian would not allow himself to be hood-winked. He lifted himself in his bed, and shouted so that the whole staff ran into the tent, while the wounded men uneasily turned their heads:

"I know it, I tell you, I know her; she is a German spy; she is the 'lady doctor'!"

The French staff captain started when he heard this nickname. "Oh!" he cried. "If you are perfectly sure of that we have made a good catch!"—and he beckoned to two surgeons who were entering the tent in order to ascertain the cause of the commotion. "Arrest that woman—she is a spy!"

In great excitement, René Austin tried to explain how he had once before unmasked this spy, when matters took an unexpected turn.

Annemarie Lesser suddenly stooped, seized the cloak of the French officer, to which his revolver-holster was strapped, sprang to the door of the tent, tore it aside, and ran for the motor-cars. The surgeons ran after her, shouting: "Stop the spy!" Two soldiers who were standing by the parked cars pulled themselves together and raised their rifles; but the fugitive, who had already thrown off her white hospital overall, dodged aside, and displaying a strength with which no one would have credited her, took a flying jump over a hedge. She fell, scrambled up, and ran ten yards to the edge of a little wood. Shots crashed behind her; they missed their mark, but they gave new strength to the fugitive's limbs. She could hear her pursuers behind her; and she rushed through the wood, with the officer's cloak thrown over her left shoulder, and his revolver in her right hand. She was running for her life. She broke out of the farther side of the wood, and in the falling twilight crossed a road, changed her direction, and ran in the direction of the gun-fire which was now plainly audible, interrupted from time to time by the distant clatter of machine-guns.

Crossing a meadow strewn with blocks of granite, she came to another wood. Before her rose some little hills, and she swiftly began to climb.

She had gone some two hundred yards when she heard her pursuers panting behind her. She turned, and saw two soldiers running after her, their rifles in their hands. She took cover behind a tree; the soldiers crossed a clearing; the woman raised her revolver, and two shots rang out. . . .

Presently someone began to climb the hill. The feet of the climber were shod in the shoes of a French soldier; the legs were enveloped in puttees; the body was wrapped in an officer's cloak; the badges of rank were torn off, as is usual in the front line; a soldier's cap was drawn over the climber's eyes. The climber quietly proceeded up the hill, and presently stopped, and looked back, and saw that a line of pickets, incited by the shouted orders of their officers, were searching the wood with blood-hounds.

Before her pursuers the "lady doctor" fled into the night. She was guided by the thunder of the guns, which grew ever nearer and nearer, and the Véry lights which illumined the darkness. She avoided the battery positions, and the provisional trenches of a company which was covering the retreat of its own regiment.

With the certainty of a sleep-walker, and with an

intuition that was almost that of a clairvoyante, she found her way through the widely-separated outposts of the French troops.

A German artillery officer, going the rounds of the infantry outposts in the early dawn, for purposes of reconnaissance, accompanied by a sergeant and an orderly, suddenly heard footsteps in the wood before him. Revolver in hand, he took cover with his men behind a stack of cut copse-wood; and suddenly he saw a French officer approaching across a clearing.

"Halt!" cried the German, ready to fire if his order was not obeyed. "Hands up!"

The officer halted immediately, and threw up his hands.

For a moment the German listened, but all was silent in the wood. With one stride he was beside the French officer. "Prisoner!" he cried.

Revolver in hand, he stood before his prisoner. And the prisoner tore the cap from her head. "Thank God!" said a woman's voice, in good German. "Take me at once to the nearest Staff!"

The officer was speechless.

"Be quick!" cried the woman who wore the uniform of a French soldier. "Be quick! I am a German spy, and I have the most important information!"

The officer was young and intelligent. He at once broke off his reconnaissance, ran back through the outposts to the front line, to the battalion staff, to the regimental staff; and presently a divisional motor-car drove quickly to the rear, and before a staff officer of the

Army Corps a woman dressed in a French uniform fell in a dead faint.

Two hours later, by the time an officer of the General Staff had arrived, the "lady doctor" confronted him across a table covered with maps. A nursing sister had given her a dress, and a surgeon had listened to her confession. An injection of morphia had quickly restored her energies. What the spy had to report to the two officers of the General Staff filled them with consternation. On all parts of the Western front fresh troops were moving forward, well armed, well equipped, well fed; and the reserve forces of the French armies consisted of American troops in unsuspected numbers, well rested and in high spirits. Working with a skilful pencil on the maps outspread on the table, the "lady doctor" indicated all that she had learned on her journey from south to north behind the French lines. When she had finished the map showed the movements of the French troops behind the front; the flank marches were no longer a carefully guarded secret; and it was evident where the enemy intended to make his final counter-offensive.

The two officers turned pale as they were forced to realize the tremendous man-power of the enemy. The General Staff officer knew who this woman was who was now sitting before him; he knew that he was dealing with the greatest and most reliable of the German secret agents; he knew that her information, terrible as it was, would be correct even to its details.

An aeroplane carried Annemarie to the Great Headquarters. There once more she put on paper all the details of her report, and the information which she had brought was at once forwarded to the General Staff officers of all the higher commands of the Western Army.

When the "lady doctor" returned to the familiar rooms of the house in Königgrätzer Strasse Matthesius could not conceal his delight and his emotion. As they sat together during the night, while Annemarie expounded the results of her reconnaissance, Matthesius, too, changed colour. This man, who had half a lifetime of experience in drawing conclusions from the reports of his agents, felt an icy chill in his very bones as he examined his colleague's notes. He saw all too clearly what must presently happen on the Western front.

While the Armistice was being concluded, and when the rattle of rifle-fire that announced the revolution was heard even in the quiet rooms on the third floor of the house in Königgrätzer Strasse, Matthesius and Annemarie Lesser burned their papers. Maps, portfolios, files, pencils and compasses followed their papers into the flames of their great fireplace. The game was lost.

At first the "lady doctor" remained in her rooms. And one day Matthesius, to whom quiet and inactivity were a physical poison, informed her that he was leaving for Budapest. Wrangel's "Whites" had for some time had their headquarters there; and there the political adventurers of every country had their rendezvous. And from Budapest he too had received an offer of a post which would enable him to continue the work which had grown to be his very life. He begged Annemarie Lesser to accompany him thither. She refused. She sat for hours on end before the open fire, staring into the flames. Now, for the first time in many years, she inquired what had become of her father. She learned that he was dead, and that the family inheritance—which, of course, meant nothing to her now—was scattered to the winds.

One day an ex-officer who had held a high command in the German Army entered the now deserted and neglected house in Königgrätzer Strasse. He told Annemarie that it was he who, years ago, had introduced Carl von Wynanky to Matthesius, and that he now felt it was his moral duty to do what he could for her.

Annemarie Lesser took a small house, which stood in the midst of a garden, in the suburb of Zehlendorf. The doctors did their best for this woman, who appeared to have no friends or close relations. At first it seemed that they would be able to help her, but it proved to be too late. Morphia and cocaine and mental stress had ruined her nervous system, and one day, accompanied by foreign nurses, she left Berlin for Switzerland. There, in the midst of an exquisite landscape, stands an asylum for mental cases, within whose walls she lives to-day. Her mind is clouded, her intellect destroyed. From time to time, on nights when the mountain wind wails around the house, tearing at the doors and windows, she suddenly begins to shriek aloud.

It is all that the nurses can do to restrain the raving woman. Name after name she shrieks into the night; it seems as though she is trying to save a man whose name is Coudoyanis from the rifles of the French soldiers; or she seems to be fighting with soldiers who are pursuing her through a wood; or she weeps, and then, it may be, she is standing, in the spirit, before a grave, and the stone above the grave bears the name of Carl von Wynanky.

And the walls of the asylum are themselves a living tomb; the tomb of the greatest of the German spies who served their country in the Great War.

CHAPTER EIGHT

A GREAT SPY

IN the whole history of European warfare no
instance of espionage was ever attended by such
stupendous results as that in which the British
spy, Alexander Szek, was concerned. The activities of
this young man had such repercussions on the fate
of the peoples of Europe that it was in no small
measure due to him that the Great War was won by
the Allied Powers. In the course of this affair the
British secret service achieved a *coup* of such importance
that in the whole history of espionage in all times and
countries it would be hard to find its equal.

At the end of February, 1917, Reuter's Agency
announced that even before the entrance of America
into the war the text of a letter from the German
Secretary of State, Zimmermann, to the German Minister in Mexico, von Eckhard, was known not only in
the United States, but in all the allied countries. According to Reuter, the text of the letter was as follows:

"BERLIN,
"19th January, 1917.
"On February 1st we shall begin the unrestricted
U-boat warfare. Nevertheless, it is our intention to

keep America neutral. If our efforts in this direction
fail, we propose an alliance with Mexico, on the following basis: that we make war and conclude peace in
common. We should guarantee general financial support, and it will be taken for granted that Mexico will
recover the lost provinces of New Mexico and Arizona.
The details of the treaty will be left to you. It is for
you to sound Carranza in the strictest confidence, and so
soon as it is certain that war will break out with America,
to intimate to him that he should, on his own initiative,
get into touch with Japan, inviting the co-operation of
that country, and at the same time offering to negotiate
between Japan and Germany. Direct Carranza's attention to the fact that the waging of the unrestricted
U-boat warfare makes it possible to force England to
her knees and bring about a peace within a few months.

ZIMMERMANN."

The publication of this letter roused an outburst of
indignation throughout the world. It was believed that
Germany had been guilty of a military conspiracy
against a still neutral country, and that she was attempting to induce Japan to take part in the war against
America. The press, which in America was in favour
of the war, now began to paint the Japanese peril (always regarded as latent in South America) in alarming
colours. It was said that American army leaders had
always been aware that if Japan were ever to make an
attack upon the United States, this attack would probably be made, through Mexican territory, upon the

Mississippi valley, in order to divide the country in two. The most important result was, of course, that the Government of the United States, which had been acquainted with the text of this letter from the very first —that is, in January, 1917—now directed all its energies to bringing America into the war.

For the Federal Government this was a difficult situation, for since both France and Great Britain had the text of the letter, and since they might at any time make it public, it was an easy matter for both these countries to bring extreme pressure to bear, through the public opinion of the United States, on the Federal Government. The American press was extremely touchy in matters relating to the Mexican frontier, and if, in addition to the Mexican bogy, the Japanese peril was invoked, the Government, unless it took action, would obviously be in the most critical situation.

Only after the facts had been published by Reuter's Agency did the general public realize that the text of Zimmermann's letter had fallen into enemy hands. In Germany the incident had an extremely depressing effect. Zimmermann, directly the fact became known, made a declaration before the committee of the Reichstag. He said that it was quite impossible to understand how the Americans could have obtained the text of the letter, which was written in an absolutely secret cipher. In the Reichstag there was a lively and perplexed discussion of all the possibilities of the case. The Secretary of State had not explained how the message to the German Minister in Mexico had been forwarded. The general belief was that it had been sent by letter post. Georg Bernhard contributed a leading article to the *Vossische Zeitung*, in which he stated:

"In the press the opinion has been openly expressed that the letter was stolen from a courier of the German Legation on the way to Mexico. Such a possibility may be excluded from the outset. We cannot imagine that such a message was ever given in written form to a courier, however reliable."

Georg Bernhard did not then know how completely his assumption was justified. The instructions of the Secretary of State were not contained in a letter at all; they were communicated in quite a different way.

During the early days of the German invasion of Belgium an officer of the Brussels command took up his quarters in an old aristocratic mansion. The house was the property of a very wealthy Austrian manufacturer, Herr Szek, who lived there with his wife, an Englishwoman, and his young son, Alexander. The officer had been hardly a few hours in the house when Alexander Szek introduced himself to him and made him the following announcement: He told the officer that he had been experimenting in wireless telegraphy; that he had constructed a receiving apparatus, and that the house was equipped with an aerial. He begged that the officer would transmit his notification to the Brussels command, so that he should not be suspected of indulging in wireless espionage.

The officer reassured the young man, inspected his apparatus, and on the following day told the competent officer—he was an officer of a wireless signalling corps —what he had seen and what Alexander Szek had told him.

The officer of the signalling corps called at the house and remained there for some hours. He stated that Alexander Szek had succeeded in constructing receivers of a quality as yet unknown in the German Army. Above all, he had devised an apparatus of a kind which in those days was something quite new, which was capable of receiving almost any wave-length, from the shortest to the longest.

The officer reported what he had seen to his superiors, and asked himself, privately, whether this young man, who appeared to have such an extraordinary knowledge of the technique of wireless reception, could not be somehow enabled to make practical use of his knowledge.

The military authorities in Brussels now made, in secret, very searching inquiries concerning Alexander Szek. They learned that his father, a very wealthy Austrian manufacturer, had moved in the highest circles of Viennese society, and was well known at the Austrian Court. He was famed for his strongly nationalistic sentiments, and was regarded, politically, as more than reliable. The mother, an Englishwoman by birth, had adapted herself to Austrian ways, and from the political standpoint was regarded as being, at all events, quite above suspicion.

The result of these inquiries was that influential Austrians, whose attention had been drawn to them, asked the Military Government of Brussels the reason of their interest in the Szek family. The German authorities asked in return whether they could employ the young man in a position in which important military secrets would become known to him. The answer they received was: "Unquestionably."

Thus it came to pass that Alexander Szek was requested to place himself at the disposal of the German authorities. He at once consented to do so, for his political sentiments, at this stage of his career, were the same as his father's. He was employed in a civilian capacity, and was appointed, at first, to a not very important post in the wireless receiving station of the German administration in Belgium. Here, to begin with, his duties consisted in the erection of receiving apparatus, and since his extraordinary technical abilities were obvious from the first, he was presently entrusted with the task of supervising the continuous reception of messages in different wave-lengths.

Alexander Szek was before long a man in whom his superiors had the greatest confidence, and it was inevitable that he would soon be promoted to one of the highest posts which the service had to offer. In this wireless receiving station all sorts of extremely important messages were constantly being received; the official messages of the German Government and the telegrams of the Great General Staff. Every precaution was taken to prevent these messages falling into enemy hands. They were one and all transmitted in a code which was kept strictly secret. The code-book was in the possession only of the highest officials of the German Government, and the organizations subordinate to them. In order that no misuse should ever be made of the code-book none but the most important official telegrams were sent by this most secret code. Since telegrams of this importance were transmitted to only a very few recipients—to the Great General Headquarters, the Governor-Generals, and the foreign embassies and legations of the Imperial Government—the code-book was in the hands of only a very few officials, who had, of course, to guard it with the greatest secrecy.

This important key had been elaborated in time of peace at the cost of endless labour. It consisted of two volumes, one large thick book and one much smaller. The thick volume contained the individual letters of the alphabet in numerals, and entire words were also expressed in numbers. But the whole volume was useless without its companion. This second volume explained that on each day of the year the basic numerals had to be altered, and in such a way that even after the basic numbers for the different days in the year had been ascertained they had to be subjected to certain manipulations in conjunction with numbers given in the smaller book.

This code, then, was one of those secret codes which can never be deciphered.

Before long Alexander Szek was one of the few men who were occupied, day and night, in a specially appointed room of the receiving station, with the reception of the secret State telegrams to the Governor-General of Brussels. And part of their duty was to decipher these dispatches with the aid of the code-book.

Soon after the beginning of the war Captain Trench, of the British Royal Marines, began to take an interest in this wireless station, and this interest was enormously increased when the British secret service discovered that this station was receiving State dispatches in the most secret code of the German Government, a code of whose existence the secret service was of course aware. Captain Trench now ascertained, through his agents in Brussels, the identity of the men whose task it was to decipher this code. Amongst other names he was given that of the young Austrian, Alexander Szek.

The English secret service made exhaustive inquiries respecting this young man. It learned that he had an English mother, and it thereupon consulted the military authorities in order to consider what could be done. Somehow, it seems, Admiral Sir Reginald Hall found a means of enlisting the young man's services. Precisely how he did so he has never divulged. But we know, at all events, that he succeeded in persuading friends of the Szek family in Brussels to get into touch with Alexander Szek, and we know that the negotiations were successful. When the young man heard the offer made by the British secret service he proposed one night to steal the code-book, and then, having previously made careful preparations, to escape with it over the Dutch frontier. It is known that the British secret service opposed this plan in the most decisive manner, for when the theft of the code was discovered the Germans would change the key of their cipher from one day to the next, and the theft would be rendered futile. There was consequently nothing for it but that Alexander Szek must sit himself down, on nights when he was quite alone in the receiving-station, and copy the whole of both volumes from cover to cover.

When he had done this he reported himself as sick. A doctor certified that his nerves had broken down; and his opinion was, as a matter of fact, perfectly correct. Alexander Szek himself brought the copy of the secret code to Holland. In those days the frontier was already protected by high-tension electric wires. He prepared a wooden stretcher, covered with bicycle tyres, with which he pushed the wires asunder at an unguarded spot, and crept over the frontier.

Since that moment no one has ever heard of Alexander Szek. But the code-book came safely into the possession of Sir Reginald Hall. And from that day onwards—and this was some time before the United States entered the war—the Allied Powers were enabled to receive and decipher all the State dispatches of the German Empire.

The Secretary of State, Zimmermann, did not send his instructions to the German Minister in Mexico by letter post; he dispatched them by wireless telegraph to the Mexican wireless station at Chapultepec, which forwarded them to the German Minister, who then de-coded them.

The fact that the most important code of the German Government had fallen into enemy hands was unknown to the public, and also, unfortunately, to the German authorities, until the press of the enemy countries divulged the facts after the war.

The fate of the traitor Alexander Szek is to this day a mystery. He has simply disappeared. His father expended large sums of money and employed private detectives in his endeavours to find his son. They discovered only one trace of his movements. The trail led from Belgium to England. When the young man's father learned, from the details published in the foreign press, the motives which had led to Alexander's disappearance, he wrote a despairing letter to Admiral Sir Reginald Hall, imploring the Admiral to tell him what had become of his son. Sir Reginald Hall replied that he had never heard the name of Alexander Szek.

Logic may help to explain a conceivable reason for the disappearance of Alexander Szek. If he had continued to live he might, in a weak moment, during the course of the war, have revealed the fact that he had stolen the code for the British Government. If this fact had come to the ears of the German Government the code would have been worthless, for it could readily be altered. A weapon essential to the final winning of the war would have been lost. If Alexander Szek died before he could reveal his knowledge there could be no danger of such a loss.

The North British newspaper, *The Scotsman*, reported in its issue of 21st November, 1925, that Lord Balfour, in an address delivered before the University of Edinburgh, referred to the betrayal of this code. Lord Balfour stated that it was an astonishing fact that no one had ever been rewarded for this betrayal, for "this stupendous service" rendered to the Allies.

CHAPTER NINE

MATA HARI: DANCER, COURTESAN AND SPY

CAPTAIN MACLEOD of the Dutch Army sat in the tea-room of the Hôtel des Indes in The Hague, gazing, with a bored expression, through the window, into the wide *place* which lies before the hotel. It was the winter of the year 1894. Early in the afternoon the snow had begun to fall, and the captain was beginning to feel tired of watching it. Macleod had published a matrimonial advertisement; he was looking for a wife, whose dowry would enable him to settle down. He had received a letter from a man who suggested that his daughter would perhaps be the wife for him; she would receive a respectable dowry, and was young, handsome, and of a cheerful disposition. Captain Macleod sat in the Hôtel des Indes and waited for his first interview with this young woman, and he shuddered a little as he reflected that she would probably be some thick-set tradesman's daughter, devoid of physical charm, and that nevertheless he might have to marry her.

The captain suddenly sprang to his feet; so utterly amazed that he upset his teacup, and knocked a plate off the table, which was followed by the sugar basin, for there, before the confused and blushing soldier, whose face revealed his measureless astonishment, stood a young girl, of such beauty that Macleod, though a widely-travelled man of much experience, had never seen the like. She was of medium height, slender but well-proportioned; her limbs displayed the most perfect symmetry; her skin had a golden tint; her black eyes were exceptionally large, and her thick, black, rebellious tresses framed a classic profile. Such was Margheretha Zelle as she stood in the tea-room of the Hôtel des Indes, smiling at the officer and the disorder of his tea-table. It was a few moments before Macleod was able to realize that this divine creature, at whom all the guests in the tea-room were gazing in admiration, was the lady who, according to her father's letter, might become his wife for the asking.

An hour later Margheretha Zelle took her leave of the captain, for whom this hour had seemed but a minute; and she had hardly disappeared when Macleod rose, threw some money on the table, ran through the streets, climbed the dark and grimy stairs of a shabby house, rapped violently on the door of an advertisement bureau, once more threw some money on the table, and learned, in answer to his questions, that Margheretha Zelle, born at Leeuwarden, the principal town of Friesland, was the daughter of a man who was either a Javanese or a half-breed, but had married a Dutch wife, and was now the proprietor of a prosperous hat shop. Margheretha's parents were well-to-do; the mother was related to families of the Dutch nobility; the daughter was born in 1880, and was therefore fourteen years of age. The extraordinarily precocious physical development of the girl was doubtless explained by the fact that her father was not of pure European descent.

On the 30th March, 1895, there was a fashionable wedding in Amsterdam: Margheretha Zelle became the wife of Captain Macleod. Thanks to the presence of Macleod's relations, officers of high rank, many of whom were the bearers of noble names, and the kinsfolk of the bride's mother, it was a wedding that attracted some attention in fashionable Dutch society. All were unanimously agreed that the bride was the loveliest girl who had ever been seen in Dutch society, not excluding the Court. The newly-wedded pair began their married life in Borneo, and after a time proceeded to Sumatra, and then to Java, as shortly after his marriage the captain was once more stationed in tropical garrisons. The captain's wife, surrounded by numerous servants, lived a life of her own; she steeped herself in the native literature, and accepted the doctrines of the Buddhist faith. Her first child, a boy, died suddenly soon after his birth, and the young mother was plunged into despair. A second child of the marriage survived: a girl, Jean Louise. Margheretha lived in an unreal world, spending more and more time in the temples of the native quarters in which she remained for hours at a time.

The marriage was not a happy one. The captain fell a victim to the fever of the country. Violent scenes were not unusual now, and one day there was an open scandal; the European neighbours had to intervene, and the captain's superior officers were obliged to take action. One night Captain Macleod sat drinking on the open verandah of his house; he sent for some native women of worse than dubious reputation, and then, entering his wife's bedroom with a horsewhip in his hand, he threw her out of bed and forced her to witness an orgy such as would be unthinkable outside these tropical islands.

A few days later the captain, with his wife and daughter, sailed for Europe. Macleod was transferred to Amsterdam. His pay was insufficient to meet the expenses of life in the Dutch capital; the social position of the Macleods had suffered as the result of the scandal, and the captain began to live a wild and dissolute life. One night he turned his wife into the street, telling her to get money—how and where was no concern of his.

His wife obtained the money that night. But some little time later there came a day when Macleod, leading his little daughter by the hand, left the house, in which a policeman was stationed, in accordance with the Dutch law, until the mortgaged furniture was redeemed or removed.

Mevrouw Macleod went to her father, and while she stood behind his counter, selling hats, or mended the clothes of the household in the evenings, or swept and dusted the house, she formed a resolution which may perhaps be explained by her exotic origin, and by the

young and beautiful woman's thirst for life and enjoy-
ment, a longing restrained by none of the usual inhibi-
tions. Margheretha took the money which she found
in her father's till, and boarded the train for Paris. It
was the beginning of a journey from which none has
ever returned.

One evening, destitute and half starving, she was
standing in a dark gateway of a narrow street. A
woman of the streets gave her a piece of advice:

"*Ma petite*, you are still young and beautiful: you
could manage something better than this life. I know
a house where they'd be delighted to take you in, young
and pretty as you are. Will you give me three francs
if I take you there?"

The woman who was once Mevrouw Macleod al-
lowed herself to be escorted to a *maison publique* in the
Quartier Latin. When she rang the door-bell an old
and faded woman appeared, who showed her then and
there into a bedroom. It was gaudily furnished, in the
most execrable taste; in the middle of the room was a
broad, low bed, whose canopy was lined with mirrors.
In this room Margheretha spent the summer. This
was such a high-class establishment that the ladies who
inhabited it were not required, week after week, to pay
their regulation visit to the sanitary police; but Monsieur le docteur Bizard, who was the surgeon of the
women's prison of St. Lazaire, came to the house at the
prescribed intervals, and examined the inmates.

With the coming of winter the *jeunesse dorée* returned to the capital; Margheretha rose a little in the

demi-monde, and then came the great transformation: from the inmate of a brothel to the *grande cocotte,* the fashionable courtesan. She took a beautifully furnished house in Neuilly; the house, the furniture, her dresses and her carriage were provided by a wealthy manufacturer, who left his wife and children in order to live with her. She accompanied her lover to the small and delightful watering-places of the Côte d'Azur, and while she was in Nice she heard that her former husband, Captain Macleod, was dead. He had left nothing but a number of debts and his little daughter. Some time later she woke one morning in her own house, and when she opened the morning paper she read that her lover had been arrested; he had forged cheques, squandered his property, and ruined himself for his mistress. And now, for some months, no one heard of Margheretha. But one day her aristocratic clients were surprised by receiving cards of invitation for an evening in October (the year was 1905). Margheretha was entertaining her friends in the Musée Guimet, the meeting-place of the Orientals in Paris. She invited not only her clients, but the most celebrated Orientalists, men of letters, artists, and journalists. The invitations announced that an Indian dancer would give an exhibition of temple dances, and the name of the dancer— printed in blazing red letters on a black ground—was "Mata Hari." Only the initiated knew that this name consisted of two Malay words: Mata, "the eye," and Hari, "day"; the whole being a picturesque Malay expression for the sun; and that this name concealed the personality of Margheretha Zelle, once the wife of Captain Macleod. The fiction of the "Indian dancer" was so well maintained, and so effectively broadcast, that the hall was literally full to overflowing.

Her success was immediate, stupendous, and overwhelming; such as would not have been possible elsewhere than in the readily enthusiastic Paris of the years before the war. To judge by the reports of contemporaries, and the criticisms in the Parisian newspapers, which advertised the success of the hitherto unknown dancer to the world, her performance must have been truly extraordinary. For the dances which Mata Hari performed on the stage of the Musée Guimet were no mere choreographic rhythms; her dance was one magnificent intoxication of the senses, whose focus was a woman of classic loveliness and fascinating charm. To the exotic clangour of Oriental music, or to the accompaniment of the most refined of modern tone-poems, against a background of genuine Malayan or Oriental decorations, this woman danced a series of dramatic episodes, and her body, lithe and expressive beyond words, mirrored so marvellously the classic joy in sensuality, the eager affirmation of life and love, that the spectators were beside themselves with enthusiasm.

From this day onwards the name of Mata Hari echoed through all Europe. No one pried into her past; all were convinced that a divinely gifted dancer was making her first appearances. Triumph followed upon triumph. Before long the Paris theatres—the Théâtre Marigny in the Champs Élysées, the Folies

Bergères and the Scala—were bidding against each other, offering sums of transatlantic magnificence, for the dancer who could have filled the house twice over. Mata Hari was now the foremost dancer of the day, and for many months she maintained her supremacy, despite the appearance in Paris of Otero, Ida Ruben-stein, Regina Badet and Isadora Duncan. Her fantastic success in Paris was followed by a triumphal progress through the capitals of Europe.

And one night, on her return to Paris, as she left the stage of the Folies Bergères after an unprece-dented artistic triumph, she found, before the door of her dressing-room, a tall, fair, elegant man who had the look of a conqueror. In his arms he bore a huge bouquet of priceless orchids. This man, whom she had never seen before, smiled at her, and spoke a few words, and his whole person was so uncon-cerned, so compelling, so victorious, that it never entered the dancer's mind to resist him. Next morning she woke to find him beside her in the vast bed that occupied the centre of her bedroom. This man was the Marquis Pierre de Montessac, a luminary of the nocturnal heavens of Paris, an *arbiter elegantiae*, the friend and confidant of the wealthy and aristocratic officers of the Garde Républicaine. Long afterwards the French police found in Mata Hari's possession letters which were directed to a Marquis P——. Dur-ing her trial every effort was made to discover who this man really was, what he had done, and what was his origin. But in the days of Mata Hari's triumph no one in Paris troubled his head about such matters. The man was there; he was wealthy, smart, and an aristocrat; he was punctual in the payment of his heavy gaming debts, and amidst the *jeunesse dorée* of the day he was a man who was taken at his word. It was long before the real identity of this man was discovered. It was not known until the year 1927, when a Mr. Netley Lucas decided to become an honest man. Mr. Lucas was for some decades a distinguished ornament of the criminal world of Paris; a man whose profession was the perpetration of exquisite forgeries; an expert safe-breaker, a mysterious hotel thief. Mr. Lucas paved the way to a life of tranquil respectability by writing a book in which he recorded his misdeeds. In this book, whose details have been confirmed by the police, and which is completely trustworthy, the author speaks of a certain Comte Pierre, who is identical with the Marquis de Montessac. No one, says Mr. Lucas, knew where the Marquis came from, but he spoke excellent Russian, English, French, and German; and as he spoke each of these languages as though it had been his mother-tongue, no one knew what was really his native language. He had studied in Bonn, and while he was still a student his father died somewhere on the French Riviera, leaving him a large fortune, the last remnants of which he lost at Monte Carlo. But he could not bid farewell to his luxurious style of living; he lived, as before, the life of a wealthy man of fashion, but he never left any of the hotels which he patronized without taking with him some memento.

After his departure some of the guests invariably found that their valuable jewels or well-filled pocket-books were missing. Although he was never detected, he wearied of this way of life, and one day—in Lausanne, it is believed—an agent of the German Intelligence Service made him a certain proposal. This proposal he accepted. The Marquis de Montessac, once more abundantly supplied with money, appeared in Paris. Before long, as we have seen, he was the friend of all the officers of the Garde; and he was a man who, when he rode or drove through the Bois de Boulogne, aroused the enthusiastic appreciation of all connoisseurs of fashion. He was always to be seen at the great flying events; he took a course of instruction as pilot, and his friends were convinced that he did so for no other reason than that aviation was *le dernier cri*. He was not always in Paris; he made brief excursions to almost every country in Europe; not always as the Marquis de Montessac, but sometimes as the Russian Captain Mazaw Marzaw.

When he returned from one of his journeys in July, 1914, Mata Hari hurriedly sold her villa at Neuilly, with all its luxurious appointments, and her château, which had once belonged to La Pompadour, and suddenly, quite without warning, she disappeared from Paris.

During the first days of August, 1914, Mata Hari appeared in Berlin, in the principal theatre of varieties.

A few days later she had once more disappeared. She was now accompanied by an inconspicuously dressed manservant, who carried her trunk. When they were alone they conversed as intimates, and in Amsterdam they parted.

A few days later the Marquis de Montessac reappeared in Paris. He was warmly greeted by his friends; he paid many calls; he pulled every possible string, and presently he attained his object: having already had some experience as an aviator, he was enlisted in the French Flying Corps. After a short period of instruction he obtained a commission. He was not a pilot, but an observer, and later on he was given an administrative post, and as Mr. Lucas tells us in his book, he devoted himself to picking up items of information which might be of service to Germany.

For a time Mata Hari remained in Amsterdam. She lived a life of great retirement, visited by none of her former acquaintances; once or twice she crossed over to London, returned, and suddenly reappeared in Paris. But the British Intelligence Service had become suspicious of her. She was watched while in London, but nothing whatever was discovered which gave reason to believe that she was a spy, and the authorities confined themselves to informing the French secret service that she was under observation. When she returned to Paris she resumed her old way of life. She became the mistress of a man who held a high position in the French Foreign Office, and she immediately paid a visit to the Marquis de Montessac, who was on duty in an aviation camp. Once more she appeared in public, and Paris, which had not seen her for many years—for this was

in the summer of 1916—welcomed her return with
enthusiasm. Suddenly she decided to devote herself
to the care of the wounded. She applied for a pass to
Vittel, as she wished to work in the hospital there. At
Vittel one of the principal aerodromes of the French
Army had recently been constructed. She did, as a
matter of fact, nurse the wounded in this hospital, but
at night she was entertained by the officers of the Flying
Corps; she was toasted, admired and desired. Suddenly her money gave out. She returned to Paris.
She had hardly arrived when detectives entered her
hotel and requested her to accompany them to the
bureau of the French counter-espionage service. There
she was taken before Captain le Doux, the head of the
home branch of the service.

Captain le Doux did not rise from his chair as the
dancer entered his office.

"You will leave France immediately. All the allied
Powers are suspicious of you. It is feared that you
may be acting as a spy, and I wish you to return at
once to your native country, to Holland, and not to
enter France again for the present."

"*Mon Dieu*, but how did such an idea ever enter
your head?"

"This idea is not wholly unrelated to the many connections which you have formed in Paris, and above
all, with the many acquaintances which you have made
among officers of the Flying Corps."

No one knows what was the rest of the conversation
between the dancer, Mata Hari, and Captain le Doux;

there were no witnesses to the conversation, but one thing is certain: when Mata Hari left the bureau of the counter-espionage service she had been given permission to remain in France only on condition that she now acted as a spy for the French authorities. We know also that the French Intelligence Service was not as yet aware that Mata Hari was sending information to Germany by devious routes, and that the Marquis de Montessac had long been acting as a German spy. This they first learned from the reminiscences of the man who wished to settle down to the life of a respectable citizen, and who therefore, in order to make things easier for himself, divulged a few little matters to the police.

Mata Hari left Paris for an unknown destination. Somewhere she met Montessac; then, proceeding to Amsterdam, she disappeared completely, to reappear later in Paris. Early one morning she appeared before Captain le Doux. During the same morning two large French destroyers, which were cruising in the Mediterranean, suddenly altered their course; a few large submarines joined them, and two German submarines, which lay at anchor off the coast of Morocco, were that evening surprised by the French flotilla, torpedoed, and sunk. What had Mata Hari to do with this matter? It was she, an agent of the German secret service, who betrayed these German submarines to the French. During the course of her trial it was proved that she had received a very large sum of money for this betrayal. Was it only the money that tempted her?

It was rather the wish to remain in France at whatever cost, and she had a special reason for wishing to remain. In the French hospital at Vittel Mata Hari had come to know a Russian officer, both of whose eyes had been destroyed by a bullet. It is known that the dancer was in love with this man; and it is possible that this was the first time in her life that she had ever felt a genuine and passionate love, and that she loved the blind man for himself alone. The only explanation of her behaviour is that she was ready to do anything in order to escape banishment from the side of the man she loved, who had in the meanwhile been brought to Paris. We must remember that unrestraint was the very basis of her character. If she made money by remaining in France, so much the better; after all, what concern of hers were the terrible things that were happening all over Europe? It is true that she herself took a hand in controlling these terrible things, but only in order to earn the money which she required for her new way of life; and if she received this money from both sides at once, so much the better. Neither France nor Germany was her home, and she did not or would not believe that her duplicity might cost her her life. The woman who was accustomed to see ministers and deputies and distinguished officers at her feet could not believe that there were men in France who would demand her life. The Marquis de Montessac knew nothing of her treachery; he learned of it only at her trial. Meanwhile she continued to work for Germany in co-operation with the unsuspecting marquis. She was able to give him much important information, relating principally to the plans of the French air forces; she also kept an eye on the political situation in France, and the progress or otherwise of the movement in favour of peace by negotiation.

Towards the end of the year 1916 the French Intelligence Service learned that there was a woman in Paris who was acting as a spy for Germany, and with quite extraordinary success. The Intelligence Service was immediately convinced that this must be the woman who was known to the world of international agents by the nickname of the "lady doctor," and whose fate has been recorded in an earlier chapter. The officers of the French Intelligence Service made every possible effort to arrive at certainty in the matter, but it soon became obvious that their supposition was incorrect. For some time they knew the precise whereabouts of the "lady doctor"; she was in Berlin, yet information was reaching Berlin from Paris, which, so the French agents in Berlin insisted, was furnished by a woman. It was then that Mata Hari began to be once more suspected, and the French General Staff resolved to arrive at certainty in the matter.

Captain le Doux sent for the dancer. He gave her five letters, which were addressed to five men who were living inconspicuously in the midst of the civilian population of the occupied area of Belgium, and who were in reality French spies. The letters were sealed, but the envelopes were precisely addressed. The captain reminded the dancer that she had been given permission to remain in France only on condition that she worked for France, and instructed her to make use of her influential connections in Holland in order to procure facilities to enter the occupied area and deliver the letters. For this service the dancer was promised a considerable sum of money, and she was then and there given a respectable sum in advance.

Mata Hari had hardly left the captain's room when a French officer entered it. He was the Comte de Chilly, who was taken prisoner by the Germans, when severely wounded, in 1915. He was exchanged, and evacuated into Switzerland, where he spent some time in hospital.

He was nursed by a German Sister, Hanna Wittig, the daughter of a veterinary surgeon, who had herself studied medicine in Switzerland. The patient and his nurse fell hopelessly in love with one another, and when the Comte de Chilly left the hospital and settled in Lausanne for a time, in order to complete his convalescence, Hanna Wittig accompanied him. Lausanne was then the centre of French and German espionage. In this city were the great central organizations of both the French and German secret services, and when the more important agents returned from their adventures, or embarked on fresh ones, they passed through Lausanne. The Comte de Chilly, on account of his wound, was debarred from further service at the front; but he was an ardent patriot, and it occurred to him that he might still serve his country as a spy. Hanna Wittig, a young woman of romantic temperament and impulsive resolutions, who was attracted by the perilous nature of the undertaking, encouraged him in his intention, and even before the Comte had laid his proposal before his military superiors she began to do what she could to facilitate its realization. She stripped off her nurse's costume, transforming herself into an extremely pretty and rather extravagantly dressed young woman, and began to haunt the cafés and restaurants and tea-shops of Lausanne. And one day, by an unlikely accident, she overheard a conversation. Two men were conversing in the restaurant of an hotel. They were speaking German. Suddenly Hanna Wittig overheard a letter and a number: H 21; and then a certain item of information was alluded to which was of great importance to Germany.

The amateur spy at once left the hotel and went to the Comte, who was startled by what she had to tell him. The information which Hanna Wittig had overheard was of special interest to her lover. The Comte by chance had learned that the gist of this information, which referred to an intended movement of large bodies of troops, which movement was being kept strictly secret, had been betrayed to the Germans. This had been reported by French agents in Charleville, the site of the German headquarters. It now seemed probable to the Comte that a spy whose official number was H 21 had secured this information in France and had transmitted it to the Germans. It was important, the Comte concluded, to ascertain if his theory was correct. He at once proceeded to Paris, accompanied by his

mistress, and went straight to Captain le Doux, entering his room a few moments after Mata Hari had left
it. Captain le Doux was overjoyed when he heard
what his visitor had to tell him. H 21 must certainly
be the spy who had betrayed the information in question. Now, it seemed, they were on the right track;
they knew at least the official number of the spy.

And here something must be said of these secret
numbers. They had to be introduced into the telegrams
which poured in from all parts of the world to the
central intelligence bureaux of the various belligerent
countries. They could easily be interpolated in an
unsuspicious-looking text—for example, as the code
designation of a particular quality of goods—and the
intelligence officer who received the telegram knew at
once from whom it came, even if the signature was
that of some unsuspicious private person, or some respectable commercial firm. So many agents were employed that it was, of course, necessary to make a
written list of their names and numbers. But the fact
that such secret information had to be committed to
writing involved a certain danger of discovery.

Captain le Doux immediately wrote his instructions,
to be forwarded to his secret agents in Berlin, to the
effect that they were to discover, at all costs, the identity
of H 21.

Having done this, he turned again to his visitor,
who unfolded his proposal to become a spy. He mentioned the existence of Hanna Wittig, who had secured
the piece of information which the· two had just been

discussing, and he was asked to call again on the following day, accompanied by his German mistress. Hanna Wittig made an excellent impression on the captain. She appeared to be intelligent and adaptable, and devoid of the pronounced characteristics which are such a serious handicap to the secret agent, and the three sat in consultation until late into the night.

They discussed many things; and finally they decided on a plan of operations. That very night an orderly was dispatched with written instructions to Mata Hari. She was not to start on her journey for another six weeks. In six weeks Hanna Wittig was expected to accomplish her important task.

Mata Hari was in Paris. She wondered why her journey had been postponed. Late one afternoon—it was pouring with rain, and Mata Hari was feeling terribly bored—a caller was announced. The dancer had no longer a house of her own; she had taken one floor of an hotel. Mata Hari, thankful for any distraction, consented to receive the caller: a Fräulein Hanna Wittig from Switzerland.

Fräulein Hanna Wittig looked perfectly enchanting in her simple tailor-made costume. She was quite a young thing; she had not long left her boarding-school. She was very innocent, very inexperienced; and she was shortly going to be married to a French nobleman, a Comte de Chilly. Mata Hari looked at the girl with pleasure and approval. She could not imagine what this shy, charming young creature wanted of her. Hanna confided all sorts of things about herself and her engagement, and when at last she approached the motive of her call she became covered with confusion, blushed, and did not know how to proceed. Mata Hari rose to her feet, and led the child to a broad divan, and there, as the two women sat together, the young Swiss girl confessed what she wanted of the beautiful dancer. She wanted advice. She put her request into words which entirely won the older woman's heart.

"Madam," said the girl, "my future husband, the Comte de Chilly, is a nobleman, who knows life, and in his time he has certainly known many beautiful women. I am only a little *bourgeoise;* and it often happens that the Comte speaks of you; I think he must have known you at some time; and he always says that there is no one in the world who can equal you for charm and beauty. And I too have often heard of you; I know there isn't a man in society who doesn't praise your beauty and your art. And so I've come to ask you to help me. What can I do, what ought I to do, to make sure that Monsieur de Chilly will always love me, and always think me charming?"

The dancer looked at the girl in astonishment. Hanna Wittig had not miscalculated; Mata Hari, who was prouder of nothing than of her success in love, was flattered. She folded the girl in her arms, and the two spoke long together, while the rain drummed and splashed on the windows of the sunlit room.

That night the two women became friends. Hanna Wittig moved into the same hotel.

One day the Comte de Chilly, in full uniform—very dignified, very aristocratic, and a trifle reserved—called on the dancer to thank her for her kindness to his fiancée.

That evening the Comte said to Hanna: "I don't believe this woman is a spy. She is so beautiful, so charming, so gracious; as for her being a spy, I don't believe it." The Comte de Chilly became a frequent visitor in the dancer's drawing-room. He became distinctly friendly with her, without realizing that he was thereby confirming his mistress in the resolve to unmask the spy.

Mata Hari and Hanna Wittig were now inseparable. The course of instruction in the arts of love which the little Swiss girl was undergoing was extremely thorough and meticulous; and often enough Hanna sat on the edge of the dancer's bed until late into the night, listening to her friend or putting her artless questions. But Hanna Wittig was a clever girl. Circuitously, with blushing embarrassment, and with many pauses, she led the conversation, in the silence of the night, up to a very delicate subject. Was it true that Mata Hari had ever accepted payment for her love? "Don't be angry with me, dear, for asking; it goes without saying that I don't believe it; but there are people who say so. . . ."

Mata Hari answered without prolonged consideration. She told herself that in the eyes of her young friend she was a sort of goddess of love. She was unwilling to lose her halo, unwilling to allow its

brilliance to be ever so little dimmed; she rather preferred to reveal her great secret; and she whispered
to her friend that what people said of her was not true;
that she made her money in quite a different way; she
was a spy, working for the country in which her friend
had been born; she was working for Germany.

"But can you do that without danger? What do
you call yourself? Are you really telling me the
truth?"

Mata Hari, in her eagerness to ensure that her young
friend should refuse to believe what she had heard,
told her a few details of her experiences as a spy.
"Only a few people know, of course, that it is I who
obtain the information; I don't use my own name; I
am known as H 21."

By the time Hanna Wittig entered Captain le
Doux's office next morning, in order to tell him that
she had accomplished her task, that she had discovered
the identity of H 21, Mata Hari was sitting in the
Madrid express. When the officials of the counter-
espionage department inquired for her at her hotel
they learned that she had left Paris, but her destination
was unknown. At midday Captain le Doux received a
short note from the dancer, in which she stated that
as the six weeks were up she was proceeding, according
to instructions, to the occupied area of Belgium, in order
to deliver the five letters which had been entrusted
to her.

On the following day Captain le Doux received a

telegram from the French agents in Spain, informing him that the dancer had arrived at Madrid.

Mata Hari did not remain long in Madrid. She interviewed certain German officials there, and was unaware that she was being watched by the French agents. Finally she proceeded to the coast, and booked her passage to Rotterdam on the Dutch steamer *Hollandia*.

One windy night, when the dancer was fast asleep in her berth, a British torpedo-boat, following a zigzag course, approached the Dutch steamer. Signals flashed out; a boat came alongside the *Hollandia*, and a British officer scrambled on to the deck.

"Are you the captain of this vessel? You have a passenger, a dancer, Mata Hari. It is desirable that she should continue the voyage on a warship."

There was knocking on the door of the cabin in which Mata Hari lay asleep. There was some little excitement on board the *Hollandia*, some indignation, and much haste; British sailors removed the passenger's luggage, and presently Mata Hari, angry and indignant, was standing on the deck of the torpedo-boat. The British officers were pleasant and courteous; the torpedo-boat tore through the waves, and in due time arrived in an English harbour. A motor-car was waiting, and a few hours later Mata Hari was standing in Scotland Yard before the chief of police, Sir Basil Thompson, who immediately informed the dancer that she was strongly suspected of espionage, but without entering into any details which would justify the suspicion. During an examination which was continued for some hours Mata Hari fought for her life; she made no admissions, she fell into no traps, but Sir Basil Thompson could not see his way to permit her to continue her journey. At the close of the examination, when Sir Basil repeated once more that he was convinced that Mata Hari was a spy, there was a dramatic scene; the woman sprang to her feet, and cried:

"Yes, I am a spy; only, I am working not for Germany, but for France: a country that has become my second home, a country that I love!"

The conclusion of the whole affair was that Mata Hari was sent by sea, with a military escort, not to Rotterdam, but to Spain, and her journey ended at the port of Gijon. She did not realize that a French agent was close upon her heels; neither did she know that all her luggage had been most thoroughly searched, and that while she sat at dinner the agent had closely examined her clothes, and searched her whole cabin; and above all, she could not understand how it was that she, who was such a strong and healthy woman, should on one occasion, in the smoking-room of the ship feel suddenly so unwell that she actually lost consciousness. She was carried to her cabin, and left in the care of an English nurse, who completely undressed her, and passed her clothes out into the gangway, to a man who examined them inch by inch, but without result. And some time later the nurse announced that the dancer had nothing concealed on her body.

That evening, when she was fully recovered, and

sitting on deck, a wireless telegram was sent from the ship to Paris; this was at once deciphered and sent to le Doux. The captain learned from this telegram that the five letters which Mata Hari was to have delivered to the French spies in the occupied area in Belgium were no longer in her possession.

Mata Hari knew nothing of all these proceedings, which were finally to seal her fate, but went at once to Madrid. She put up at the Grand Hotel, where she secured a couple of luxuriously furnished rooms; which, curiously enough, were immediately adjacent to the rooms of the German naval attaché, von Kroon. The dancer remained for some weeks in Madrid; she spent much of her time in the society of French naval officers; she made the acquaintance of the French naval attaché, but for some reason, which she herself could not understand, no one any longer confided in her. Spain did not seem to be a country in which she was likely to accomplish anything. Suddenly her money gave out. She was often in the company of the German military attaché, but as to the incidents which were finally to seal her fate, we know nothing, since for obvious reasons those who know the facts are silent. One thing is certain: that the German naval attaché, Herr von Kroon, had occasion to assign to the dancer a large sum of money, which, strangely enough, was to be paid in Paris through a neutral embassy. He sent, from Madrid, a cipher telegram to the head of the German Intelligence Service in Amsterdam, asking him to see that "agent H 21" was paid the sum of fifteen thousand pesetas. The cheque for the money was to be drawn on a Paris bank, and agent H 21 would receive this cheque in Paris.

This wireless telegram was intercepted by the Eiffel Tower, and was submitted to Captain le Doux as a suspicious message. The key of the cipher employed by the German naval attaché in Madrid had some time previously been betrayed to the French, so that the message was at once deciphered.

Le Doux reflected. If the information which Hanna Wittig had given him was correct, Mata Hari must shortly appear in Paris. On the evening of the same day he received a message which confirmed his assumption: the secret agent who had followed the dancer from London telegraphed from the Spanish frontier to the effect that he was on his way to Paris "with convoy."

On the morning of the 14th February, 1917, the Paris police surrounded the Palace Hotel. Mata Hari had arrived from Madrid and proceeded to the hotel. The commissary, Priollet, was in charge of operations. A few minutes after seven o'clock he entered the lobby of the hotel with three detectives, introduced himself to the manager, and inquired the position of the dancer's rooms. He was told what he wanted to know, and was already half-way up the stairs when a man rushed into the lobby. In the street outside could be heard the throbbing of the engine of a powerful racing-car. The man was wearing a leather cape; he had no collar, and his hair hung in disorder over his forehead. He inquired of the porter:

"Where is Madame Mata Hari's room? I must speak to her at once."

The porter said nothing; the commissary on the stairs turned round; the manager came forward and said, with a glance at the official:

"Madame Mata Hari? The lady cannot be seen for the moment; there are some gentlemen here who have just inquired for her."

The man in the leather cloak looked up; he saw the men on the stairs; one hand flew to his heart; then he turned on his heels and left the hotel. The Marquis de Montessac leapt into his racing-car, stepped on the accelerator, and drove off in despair. He had failed to save the woman he loved; he had come half an hour too late.

Meanwhile Monsieur Priollet was knocking at a bedroom door. All was silent; he knocked a second time; no one answered. The third time he banged on the door with his fist, shouting:

"The police are here. Open, or I shall break in the door."

"Come in," replied a voice, "if you have no objection to entering a lady's bedroom!"

Monsieur Priollet turned the handle; the door was not locked; he entered Mata Hari's bedroom, with the three detectives behind him, feeling extremely embarrassed. The dancer was lying on her bed. She was completely naked, covered only by a cambric sheet. It was still dark in the room, which was lighted only by the lamp in the corridor. The commissary said:

"I am the police commissary Priollet. My instructions are to take you immediately to the police station."

The dancer raised herself in her bed, smiled at the commissary, and said:

"Do you want to take me to the police station naked? Do you really?"

She laughed immoderately, but the commissary did not share her amusement. He had received the strictest orders that once he had arrested this woman he was not to let her out of his sight for a moment. He took a chair, and remained in the room while Mata Hari dressed herself. She sang as she did so; she did her best to flirt with the commissary; she had no suspicion of what awaited her.

In the bureau of the French counter-espionage department the commissary did not trouble to question her at any length. He informed her that she was suspected of acting as a spy for Germany. He had only one question to ask, and it was an overwhelming question.

"Madame," he asked, "where are the five letters which you were to take to Belgium?"

Mata Hari did not lose countenance. She was indignant at having been arrested; she declared that the suggestion that she was a spy was monstrous; and she evaded the question, saying:

"You must know that the English went through my luggage. Telegraph to London; the letters may be there."

The commissary gave no replies to the questions of

the angry woman, who wanted to know what definite grounds of suspicion the authorities could have. Nor did he tell her that the authorities possessed the following all but fatal evidence against her: The five letters which Mata Hari was to have taken to Belgium were nothing more than a test which Captain le Doux had devised. They were addressed to five spies, but the French Intelligence Service was perfectly well aware that four of these spies had long ago been detected by the Germans, and had saved their lives only by undertaking to act as spies for Germany. They did this by acquainting the German Intelligence Service with their instructions, and by betraying their go-betweens. The fifth spy, however, was a man who had only recently entered the French service; he had hitherto done very little work, and under normal circumstances it was impossible that the Germans should know of his existence. A week after the letter addressed to him had been handed to Mata Hari the man was arrested and shot after due trial.

Mata Hari was taken to the women's hospital of St. Lazaire. She asked to see a lawyer; and twenty-four hours later she was informed that she would be tried by court martial on a charge of espionage for Germany. One of the most eminent pleaders of the Paris *parquet*, Dr. Clunet, undertook her defence. When the prison doctor first visited her cell—he was an elderly man, by the name of Bizard—he started; he looked at the prisoner closely, and knew that he had at some time examined this woman in a house of ill-fame. During her confinement at St. Lazaire Mata Hari was quiet and confident. She quickly made herself at home; she was still convinced that nothing very serious could befall her; for neither she nor her counsel knew the serious nature of the evidence which would be brought against her. In a strictly confidential interview with the prosecuting counsel, the French Intelligence Service had warned him that nothing must be divulged which might be of service to the enemy.

Very quietly and confidently Mata Hari faced her accusers. She was brought before the third Military Tribunal of Paris, on the 24th and 25th July, 1917. The Court consisted of twelve officers. The trial was conducted in such a way that the principal points of the indictment were declared by the prosecutor to have been proved by the reports of agents and the confidential depositions of a French spy. It was, of course, impossible that the proceedings of the Court should be made public.

At the outset of the trial Mata Hari may have felt that although she was in a serious position, she would still be able to draw her head out of the noose. But she soon began to realize her peril. It appeared that the Court was even aware of the amount of the payments which she had received from the German Intelligence Service. Mata Hari's defence was that she had indeed received various sums from the heads of the German Intelligence Service, but that they had not been paid for espionage. "It was not for that!" she cried. "My lovers were paying me for my love!"

At last, finding that she was hard pressed, she played a trump card: she rose to her feet, and cried:

"But, Messieurs, I have never had anything to do with espionage except on one occasion, and you ought to know what I did then: I betrayed two German submarines to you!"

The counsel for the defence sprang to his feet in consternation; he knew nothing of this story; and the president of the Court turned her own weapon against her.

"It is true," he said, "you did do that, but it is one more piece of evidence against you. You told us a little while ago that you had never discussed military matters with German officers or German spies. How, then, did you learn the position of these two submarines?"

The question was unanswerable.

At the conclusion of the case against the prisoner the counsel for the defence addressed the Court. In a masterly speech he enlarged upon the fact that all the evidence against the prisoner was in the form of the statements of secret agents who had not been brought into court. At most the prosecution had read the depositions made to the police, but no facilities had been given, during the trial, to test the truth of these statements. He asked for an acquittal. The reply of the prosecuting counsel was very brief. He demanded that sentence of death should be passed on the prisoner. The Court retired, on the evening of the second day of the trial, for a brief deliberation. Then the twelve officers re-entered the hall. The president uttered the word of command: "Attention!" The officers stood at attention, and the clerk of the court stepped forward.

"In the name of the French Nation the Military Court declares that Mata Hari is guilty of espionage and sentences her to death."

The deathly silence that followed the passing of sentence was rent by a woman's cry:

"It isn't possible, it isn't possible!"

But then she collected herself; proud and erect, she walked out firmly between her guards, and returned to her cell.

Her counsel appealed, but the appeal was disallowed. He made an application for pardon, but this was refused. In the meantime various persons of high rank, both French and neutral, interceded for the dancer, but without success. Her counsel made a personal appeal to President Poincaré, but in vain. The sentence of death was not to be revoked.

In prison Mata Hari revealed a dignity and courage which compelled the respect of all who came into contact with her. She was quiet and composed, and on the morning of the 15th October she stepped out of a motor-car and went quietly and firmly up to the post which had been made ready for her execution. Of the bullets fired at her only one found its mark; but that pierced her heart.

Hanna Wittig too is dead. After the war, as the wife of the Comte de Chilly, she became a celebrated film actress. She was known in her profession, and to the public, as Claude France. At the height of her fame she was tortured by the thought of Mata Hari's death. Two years ago, in her beautifully appointed house in the Rue de Faisanderie, she shot herself through the head.

CHAPTER TEN

SPIES IN THE CLOISTER

ANDREAS PEEKA, a captain in the Russian Army, and a Lett by birth, was during the war the head of a Russian intelligence bureau on the Eastern front. The sector for which he was responsible extended from Minsk to Riga. His headquarters were a little way behind the Russian front, at Rjshiza. On the other side of the front were his adversaries of the German intelligence bureau of the Army headquarters at Schaulen. On this sector of the Russian front the spies were extremely active. At various points of the sector the front line ran forward as far as the bank of the Danube, and between the positions of the hostile armies there were lakes, swamps and woods, through which it was possible to creep from front to front, and in some parts of the sector the outposts were separated by considerable intervals. For these reasons both the Russian and the German secret services were especially active on this sector. Here the spy was able, sooner or later, to enter enemy territory, and set to work behind the front.

Captain Andreas Peeka was a singular man. He was born in the neighbourhood of Mitau, of prosperous middle-class parents, and on leaving the gymnasium he became an officer in the Russian Army. Not far from his parents' house lived a rural policeman, and this policeman had a pretty daughter. During one of his terms of leave, Peeka, then a lieutenant, fell so in love with the girl that he married her out of hand. Even according to Russian ideas this was a *mésalliance* for an officer. Peeka resigned his commission and studied medicine; but on the outbreak of war he returned to the Army. He was soon promoted captain, and became noted for his skill in questioning prisoners. This, however, was not the only quality of his that attracted the attention of his superior officers. Peeka, as we have said, was a Lett, and it was important to humour the Letts, and to ensure that they turned a deaf ear to the German suggestions of an independent Lettish State. Here again Peeka was useful: as a Pan-Russian propagandist in the Lettish province. In the course of his work as propagandist he came into contact with German spies, whom the Germans had sent across the frontier with propagandist literature, and who had fallen into the hands of the enemy. Before long Peeka had discovered the capacity in which he could be most useful; he became the chief of the Russian espionage service over a large sector of the front. He lived in Rjshiza, occupying, with his servant, a somewhat old and dilapidated house, which stood a little way outside the town. The only things in this house which were always in good repair were the telephones installed in Peeka's large office, and the many wires that led thither. Once, apparently, the house had been a school; the rooms were all very large, but now most of them stood empty, and the wind whistled through the broken window-panes. The largest of the rooms was furnished for Captain Peeka; it contained a camp bed and a wash-stand, and in the middle of the room a number of tables were set together. These were covered with maps and papers, and on them stood the telephones. On these tables Captain Peeka lay on his stomach, tele-phoning, or listening to the receivers on his ears, and noting on the maps the information which he had ob-tained of the enemy's strength and positions.

True to the Russian tradition, he did not attempt to organize a service of isolated spies. He devoted him-self to wholesale espionage, and the nature of his activities, and the methods which he employed, were as fantastic as the man's whole character. Nevertheless —let it be said at once—his work was in other respects good, and proved to be of great service. Peeka, after all, had learned, by an excellent example, how espionage should not be conducted. The example was afforded by his adversaries of the German Intelligence Service in Schaulen. The intelligence officers in Schaulen had one day conceived a disastrous idea. Without much preparation, they had sought out the Letts among the prisoners of war, and had cautiously questioned them, in order to ascertain which of them were not especially well-affected towards Russia. These prisoners were sifted again and again, until a body of some eighty men was left, who, it was believed, regarded Russia not as a friend but as an enemy. These eighty men were removed to a special internment camp, where they were vigorously drilled. Each man was asked individually whether he was ready to work for the cause of Germany, and thereby strike a blow for the independence of Lettland. All answered in the affirmative, and were then equipped with revolvers, bombs, wire-cutters and trench-knives. With German thoroughness they were trained as bombers and mine-layers; all day long the sound of exploding bombs and mines might be heard in the neighbourhood of the intelligence bureau. All these prisoners proved to be smart soldiers; and one night, after due preparation, they were released into no-man's-land, and let loose upon the Russians. Behind the Russian front they were supposed to blow up railway transports, destroy bridges, and act as propagandists amidst the civil population.

But what they actually did was something very different. To begin with, they went off as arranged; but when the morning came they sought out the nearest Russian outpost, reported themselves, beaming with delight, to the first Russian officer they met, gave up their bombs, revolvers, trench-knives and propagandist literature, and related all that had happened to them. They were then given a long and well-earned leave, so that they might return to their wives and children; after which they rejoined their units. Months later some deserters informed the Germans of the singular result of their preparations.

Captain Peeka took this example to heart. He chose his spies more carefully than the Germans had done, and with other intentions in mind. He had inquiries made among the civilian population for men who had received a certain amount of education, and who were not entirely submerged in their lower-middle-class environment; men who for one reason or another were talked of among their neighbours. He also had people sent to him from the central intelligence bureau of the General Staff, men who had volunteered for service as spies, but he carefully examined them before making use of them. If he considered that a man was adapted to the work, and could be made to serve his particular ends, he had him brought to the dilapidated old house outside the town.

But even at this stage he employed the most startling methods. He regarded it as being of the utmost importance to convince the candidate that espionage, if properly conducted, is by no means an everyday affair, but something mysterious and mystical, something that ennobles the man who devotes himself to it. His object was to give the man from the very first the impression that it was a mysterious and perilous career that lay before him; and only if the applicant was not intimidated, only if he betrayed no trace of nervousness, only if he seemed a man for whom nothing could be too mysterious and hazardous, only then did Captain Peeka make use of him.

For example: Captain Peeka would single out a man who lived, let us say, some thirty miles from his headquarters. In the evening, when darkness had already fallen, a closed motor-car would suddenly appear be-

fore the man's house. He would be requested to step
into the car, which would then rush off into the night.
The man would try to look out of the window, but
could not, for the windows were fitted with black
opaque glass. He would try to estimate the direction
in which the car was travelling, but he could not, for
the car was apparently going round in a circle. He
would light a cigarette, and try to throw the match
out of the door, but in vain; for the door could not be
opened from inside the car. All that he knew was that
the car was travelling on top gear.

This was the beginning of Captain Peeka's recipe.
It had this advantage, that if the spy whom he had
trained was subsequently to be arrested, he would not
be able to give any information in respect of his employer, nor even to define such localities behind his
own front as he might have had to visit, for various
purposes, during his period of training.

The car in which the man was travelling towards
his new existence took a few sharp corners and came
to a standstill. The door opened. A hand guided the
man out of the car. Around him was utter darkness;
he had the feeling that the car had been driven into a
room of some sort. Still in the darkness, he was led
up a staircase, and suddenly he was standing, in a large
room, in front of Captain Peeka. He had been led up
out of the subterranean garage which the captain had
had built under the house.

The man who stood before Captain Peeka was
naturally somewhat bewildered, and he became even

more so when he had listened to the captain for a while. Peeka explained at once what was expected of the agent. He spoke always clearly and soberly, calling things by their right names; and he did not fail, on every opportunity, to call the man's attention to the fact that he was about to enter upon a perilous calling. If the new recruit showed the smallest sign of reluctance, if he had the very least misgivings, if he betrayed any symptoms of fear, Peeka pressed a button, and a man came forward who blindfolded the unserviceable novice and led him back to the car in the underground garage. Once more following a circuitous route, the car took him back to his house.

This was how Captain Peeka collected his agents. Such a method was possible only because of the enormous mass of human material at the disposal of the Russian Intelligence Service.

If the new recruit was willing to take service with Peeka, the captain explained the financial aspect of the undertaking. The agent received a considerable advance, but it was not paid to him directly: it was deposited in some locality named by himself. The man's task was always to spend a certain time in enemy territory, and then to return to Russia; and on his return a sum of money would be paid to him. It was always a considerable sum, but in individual cases it would be still further increased, in proportion to the results achieved by the spy.

Even if both parties were now agreed, it was a long while before the agent was let loose upon the enemy.

He had first of all to enter a school of espionage. The institution and organization of this school was one of Captain Peeka's many fantastic ideas. The school was established in an old monastery, which was situated in a very lonely neighbourhood; it was difficult of access, and there was no other human dwelling within miles. The few civilians who had formerly lived in the small houses round about the monastery had been promptly removed to other parts of the country.

The newly-recruited agent was once more blind-folded; he re-entered the car, which drove off into the night, and finally set him down in the courtyard of an ancient building.

Here all was deadly still. When the door of the car was opened, and the new spy alighted in the court-yard, he found himself confronted by a Russian officer of high rank, who briefly greeted him, and led him to one of the cells of the monastery, which had been con-verted into living-rooms for the students of espionage.

In this school there were always some fifty to sixty novices under training. There was never a cell empty. When a man's training was completed, and he was sent to the front, another of Captain Peeka's recruits imme-diately took his place.

Only once a day was the pupil permitted to take the air. The rest of the time he spent in the ancient build-ing. The door of his cell was opened, as in a prison, only when he rang. An orderly brought him food.

Day after day an intelligence officer spent some hours in the novice's cell, instructing him in the duties of his profession. He was taught precisely what to do and how to behave under various circumstances. The instruction began with a general survey of the enemy's lines; of the position of the individual regiments and batteries, and the nature of the defences, so far as these were known. He was then told where the several staffs were probably stationed, and where the ammunition dumps were situated; in short, everything worth knowing about the enemy that was already known. On the following morning he had to submit to his teacher a written exercise, in which he was required to reproduce, from memory, all that he had been told. He had also to prepare diagrams and sketch-maps in which the positions of the German troops were shown. If the agent had fully grasped the military situation, the instruction proceeded. He was now told precisely what it was desired to ascertain, and the various details were explained which would enable him to perceive any changes in the military situation. He was taught the significance of the various German uniforms, and the differences in the appearance of the different categories of field artillery; he was told how to tell the calibre of a gun; in short, during a course of training which lasted for weeks he was taught all that he ought to know. All this time he sat in his cell; except that he was allowed to take an hour or two of daily exercise alone in the monastery garden. He was never allowed to see the face of any other recruit.

When this part of his training was completed, he was instructed as to his behaviour in an enemy country. He was given a suit of clothes which was specially made and prepared for him; his appearance, his manner of speech, and his degree of education determined the text of the false passport with which he was provided. These papers might represent him as a native of the country now in the occupation of the Germans, or even as a German, or, if his task was to take him into the interior of Germany, as the subject of a neutral State. These papers were prepared with extraordinary care. The secret agent acquired a family; he had to learn all the names of all its members, and the details of any illnesses from which they happened to be suffering. In case the spy, who of course was to move about behind the front as a civilian, were to meet a body of troops accompanied by an officer, he was to act in a particular manner. He was instructed (the manœuvre was one of Captain Peeka's conceptions) that in such a dangerous predicament he was to squat innocently in the nearest ditch and let down his trousers, as though performing a physical necessity. As Captain Peeka very truly said, it is extraordinarily difficult to cross-examine a man in such a position.

After the spy had received many weeks' training of this character he was removed by night in Captain Peeka's blinded car. This time the journey was a long one, for the spy was being taken to a point close behind the front. In a lonely farmhouse the captain was awaiting him.

He made the spy put on a pair of motoring-goggles, of which the glass was completely opaque; then he led the man to the foremost Russian outpost. Only here did he remove his goggles, and only now was he given his bearings; so that if he were arrested he would not be able to betray any information whatever which might be of value to the enemy.

Captain Peeka showed the spy his position on a map. Now, of course, he was able at once to recognize the local situation, since knowledge of the geographical details of the two fronts had formed part of his professional training. He was told precisely where he could cross the front, and given a revolver, which he was to throw away if he got safely through the lines; and then he was ordered to go forward. Captain Peeka waited until his footsteps were no longer audible. If the man suddenly lost heart it was useless to attempt to return, for the outposts had instructions to open fire upon him at once, in order to silence, for good and all, an unreliable fellow.

The crossing of the Duna was one of the methods by which a man could penetrate the German front. There were pigskins inflated with air, and small specially-made boats with muffled oars; there were, in short, many means of penetrating the loosely-knit front.

About half the spies thus let loose on the enemy positions fell into the hands of the Germans as they were crossing the front line. What they could tell, if they were willing to speak, was very little. They all told a strange story of a mysterious man who had recruited them for their work; some of them described the school for spies; but more were silent, and nearly

all of them were shot. A few saved their lives by offering to act as spies for Germany.

If the spy was lucky, he spent some weeks wandering
about the German *étapes*. If he was intelligent he
learned all that can be learned, from the state of affairs
in an *étape*, of the composition of the troops at the
front; and this, of course, is a good deal. He was
given special instructions as to forwarding his information. In 1915 Captain Peeka's spies were required to
send their reports by post. They had to write an apparently innocent letter, and sign it as though the sender
was a Russian soldier interned by the Germans. In the
text the writer had to interpolate certain numbers; for
example, he might have to write: "Yesterday Ivan gave
me three cigars and fourteen cigarettes. He can't
smoke for the present. I was very glad to get them.
Now and again I visit my neighbour and see how his
geese are doing. I know before the war he had two
ganders and fourteen geese, and he was very pleased to
get thirty-eight eggs in all, and after forty-nine days
twenty-eight goslings were running about his yard." It
need not be explained that this letter was full of code
words; each noun and each number had its special significance.

This letter was simply posted in the ordinary way.
There were plenty of prisoners of war who were able
to move about in freedom, and were therefore able to
post such letters. The letters received a very cursory
inspection at the hands of the censors, and if regarded
as unsuspicious they were duly forwarded. The spies

had to address them to a certain person, whose address was Box 380, Riga. Later on they had to address them to Frau Zena in Dorpat. Frau Zena was the wife of Captain Peeka.

These addresses were constantly changed to avoid exciting the enemy's suspicions. When the spies had spent some weeks behind the German lines, and if they had accomplished their task, they turned homewards. Either they attempted to leave the enemy's territory as they had entered it, or they tried to escape by sea. Here again were many possibilities open to them.

They were instructed, on their return, to bring with them, in writing, all the information which they had secured and posted to the appointed addresses. They were so instructed because it was always possible that the letters might have aroused suspicion and then been intercepted. Since the best of memories would be unable to retain all the statistics and details of all kinds which the spy had accumulated during these weeks, Captain Peeka had hit on a brilliant idea. Before his departure from enemy territory the spy was to acquire a dog; if necessary he must buy one. This dog was to accompany him on his return. The spy was provided with very thin paper and a small aluminium tube. The paper he covered with his sketches and statistics; he rolled it up and slipped it into the tube, and the tube was inserted in the dog's rectum. There, for a time, no one thought of looking for it. The trick was detected only through a grotesque accident.

A sentry on a country road saw a pedlar trudging

along the road with his dog. The dog ran to the edge
of the ditch, whining piteously, and apparently anxious
to relieve itself. The pedlar, however, would not let
him stop, but dragged him along by his leash. The
sentry, who was a great lover of animals, felt angry;
he ordered the pedlar to let the dog do what it wanted.
The poor animal, which was evidently in difficulties,
finally got rid of a silvery metal tube. Since the sentry
had never heard that dogs were accustomed to excrete
such articles, he was struck with amazement, and being
an intelligent man he took pedlar, dog and aluminium
tube to the guard, and there related the incident. From
that time onwards all the military police of this sector
examined such dogs as were led about in the neighbourhood of the front by persons in civilian dress. In an
astonishing number of dogs such aluminium tubes were
discovered; and this and other things enabled the Germans to realize what an enormous number of enemy
agents were moving about behind the lines.

The Germans prepared to deliver a counter-stroke,
for it was obvious that such a state of affairs could not
be allowed to continue. But this counter-stroke was to
be delivered against the head of the organization, Captain Peeka. At first the authorities did not know how
to proceed. But then a German spy presented himself
at the central bureau, who proposed that he should venture into the lion's den, and at all costs dispose of Captain Peeka. All sorts of plans were discussed which
might enable the spy—whose name and origin are unknown to history—to carry out his mission. Then

chance came to his assistance. The German agents in England announced that a Russian spy who had been discussing certain matters with the British naval authorities was intending to enter Germany through Holland, in order to call on the Russian agents in certain German cities. Since this information was accompanied by precise details as to his appearance, the frontier officials recognized him at once, but allowed him, in accordance with their instructions, to enter the country. Only when he had crossed the frontier was he arrested. His papers and his passport were taken from him, and given to the German spy who was to seek out Captain Peeka.

One evening the German spy passed the last German outposts, reached the bank of the Duna, entered a boat, and rowed across to the Russian frontier. German soldiers who were in the secret fired their rifles, aiming at the water; the Russian outposts on the farther shore, hearing the shots, looked across the water; presently, a long way off—for the moon was shining—they saw a man approaching them in a boat; and the man, apparently a deserter, was waving a white handkerchief. When he reached the Russian shore he collapsed, as though exhausted. He told a plausible story of his escape through the German lines, and asked to be taken to the nearest officer. To the officer the whole affair seemed rather mysterious, but the stranger gave his name—that is, the name borne by the Russian spy who entered Germany by way of Holland. He begged the Russian officer to ring up the army headquarters, or at the very least the corps headquarters, explaining that he was a Russian spy who had come from England by way of Holland and Germany. The officer wènt to the telephone, the corps headquarters rang up the army headquarters, and the reply that was received was that all was in order; the man was really a Russian spy; he was a man who had done work of the greatest value, and must be treated with all consideration.

The spy asked that he might be taken that very night to Captain Peeka, as he had matters of great importance to discuss with him. The corps headquarters, being once more appealed to, gave the whereabouts of the captain; a car was brought up, and Captain Peeka received a late visitor. He was still up when the German spy rapped on the door of his house; he himself opened the door, and led his caller, when the latter had introduced himself, into his work-room. He knew the name given by his caller, but the man who had borne the name was unknown to him, fortunately for the German spy. Their conversation was brief; the German told him that he had just come through East Prussia; that he had secured the most important information as to the movements of troops, which he wished to lay before Captain Peeka, as to all appearances a comprehensive attack was to be made on the sector in which Peeka was working. First, however, he would be glad of quarters for the night, since he was completely exhausted by the hardships he had endured.

Captain Peeka led his guest to one of the empty rooms of the house, in which there was a camp bed and a few shabby pieces of furniture. Then he himself went to bed. About an hour later he woke, feeling rest-less and uneasy. Obeying an obscure premonition, he got out of bed and went out into the corridor in his socks. The house was perfectly silent. Not a sound was to be heard. The captain went softly along the corridor, and listened at the door of his work-room. He then went back to his bedroom, got his revolver, and returning to his work-room, suddenly opened the door.

On the floor of his room his guest was kneeling. He had made a bundle of all the papers on which he had been able to lay his hands, and was in the act of tying it securely. He was working by the light of a pocket flash-light, which he turned upon the door as it was opened. As he did so the light touched the table, and the captain saw that the leads of his telephones had been cut, and were dangling from the table.

Captain Peeka acted without a moment's hesitation. He raised his revolver, and shot the man down as he was rising to his feet.

When the Bolsheviks came into power the whole of the great Russian Empire was swept as by a whirlwind. Whither it carried Captain Peeka is as yet unknown.

CHAPTER ELEVEN

THE DEATH OF EDITH CAVELL

THE fate of Edith Cavell was that of a noble-hearted woman who died for her country. There is no doubt whatever that her transactions during the war inflicted appreciable damage on the German Army. When her activities to the detriment of the German Army were discovered she was tried by court martial and shot. Her last words to the clergyman who attended her were: "But this I would say, standing as I do in view of God and eternity; I realize that patriotism is not enough. I must have no hatred or bitterness towards anyone."

The fate of this woman, whose life was ended by the bullets of a firing-party, stirred the whole world. Here is her story, impartially related.

Edith Cavell died in her fiftieth year. She was a British subject, and a trained nurse. When the war broke out she was "Directrice de l'École Belge d'infirmières diplomées, rue de la Culture, Bruxelles": in other words, the principal of a training-school for nurses.

When, after the first great battles of the war, the hospitals of Brussels and the neighbourhood of the capital began to fill with the Belgian wounded, Edith

Cavell established a large private hospital for Belgian soldiers.

In a few days' time the whole of Brussels was full to overflowing with the wounded of the Allied troops, and this was still the state of affairs when the German Army occupied the capital. Not only in Brussels, but all over Belgium, so far as it was in German occupation, the Belgian wounded, whom their own units, in their hasty retreat, had been unable to remove, were being cared for in hospitals and private houses. When these men had recovered from their wounds there would be a small army of them in the rear of the enemy troops. The measures taken by the German High Command in respect of this state of affairs were simple and prac-tical. Every inhabitant of the occupied area was or-dered to report whether he was harbouring enemy wounded; and every director of a public or private hos-pital had to make a similar report. During the first days of the German occupation these wounded were collected by the German military authorities, and, ac-cording to their condition, were removed to hospitals in the interior of Germany, or to internment camps.

For the French and Belgian armies it was for two reasons of great importance to frustrate these measures as far as possible. The Dutch frontier was near at hand, and during the early days of the war many Bel-gians and Frenchmen who had for whatever reason remained in the rear of the German troops had escaped over this frontier. The measures taken by the German authorities were at once reported to the enemy intelligence services, and counter-measures were devised. These counter-measures were taken for two reasons. In the first place, it was of course desirable that the French and Belgian wounded soldiers should return to their units, as soon as they were fit for active service, as many of the wounded were officers and men of the regular armies—that is, they were trained and experienced soldiers. And the men who were wounded in the fighting of the first few days were, of course, among the best of the enemy soldiers. The second consideration was even more important. Every soldier who rejoined the ranks from the rear of the hostile army was a valuable source of information. A trained soldier would be able to give information as to the military situation of the enemy, and if it were possible to question a large number of such men, who had escaped from a great number of different localities, and to compare and supplement the data thus obtained, it should be possible to obtain information of the greatest importance.

The French Intelligence Service, accordingly, proceeded to create an organization whose purpose was to assist in the escape of such French and Belgian soldiers. Its agents, who slipped across the Dutch frontier, came to an understanding with the civil population of Belgium; above all, they found a ready hearing amongst the Belgian nobility; and the Prince de Croy and the Princesse de Croy were among those Belgians who sought to save their country in this and in many other ways. An organization was created, under the leadership of a few men and women, some of whose names were never discovered, which was so purposeful and efficient in its methods that it had soon spread all over Belgium. During the early days of the German invasion the smuggling of men over the Dutch frontier attained enormous dimensions. There had always been a great deal of smuggling over this frontier; there were footpaths and waterways known only to the initiated, who had their own methods of evading the frontier guards; and these routes were now utilized. No goods were smuggled now, but native guides, followed by whole troops of French and Belgian soldiers, made their way into Holland, and thence to the enemy armies. The crossing of the frontier, which was only a matter of evading the guards in the darkness, or in foggy weather, was, at all events in the early part of the war, the easiest part of the whole undertaking. In case of need, if the fugitives were numerous enough, and if they were confronted by the frontier pickets, they drew their revolvers and forced a passage. The work of organizing these secret convoys was much more difficult. To begin with, the wounded soldier had to be taken out of the hands of the German military authorities.

It was here that Edith Cavell was able to help. There were many patients in her hospital, and she had under her care a very large number of wounded soldiers who were lying in private houses. Under these circumstances it was inevitable that Edith Cavell should be approached at the very outset by the Belgian Intelligence Service. She was entreated to assist all wounded soldiers in her hospital, or in her care outside the hospital, to cross the Dutch frontier. England, of course, had already entered the war. Edith Cavell was an Englishwoman, and she maintained, during the whole of her trial, that her principal motive had been the following: Her Belgian friends had assured her that all those soldiers in Belgium who had remained unknown to the German authorities after a certain date would be shot on apprehension. Of her own accord she had taken a first step on her perilous path. In order to save the soldiers in her care from becoming prisoners of war she procured civilian clothing for them, and destroyed their uniforms. Having done this, she needed only to procure forged civilian passports for them, and she was able to declare that they were Belgian civilians, who could be identified as harmless citizens. She distributed the wounded in the houses of her numerous acquaintances, and wrote, for greater security, forged medical certificates, transforming wounded soldiers into sick civilians. That was the first step; but in order to procure civilian passports, and arrange for the crossing of the frontier, Edith Cavell had to work in close co-operation with the organization already mentioned.

After the war we were given a full description of this organization by a very reliable witness of its operations. The counsel who defended Edith Cavell before the court martial, an advocate of the Brussels Bar, Sadi Kirschen, described it, in the *Echo de Paris* of the 14th February, 1919, in the following terms:

"An organization was created. The soldiers from the northern departments of France applied to Prince Reginald de Croy, at his château of Belligny; he gave them money and a false passport; he was seconded by his sister, Princess Marie Elizabeth de Croy, and they were further assisted by Mademoiselle Louise Thuliez, a young Frenchwoman from Lille, who went by the name of Mademoiselle Martin."

The writer proceeds to enumerate the towns in which this organization had its representatives, and to name the local leaders.

It was this organization that assisted Edith Cavell. It supplied her with the Prince de Croy's false passports, which she distributed to her patients. This organization, whose activity was indefatigable, supplied also the forged medical certificates, in which a leg-wound became appendicitis, and a head wound erysipelas. The German authorities could not possibly have every sick man in the whole of the occupied area of Belgium examined in order to determine the nature of his malady, so that the medical certificate was only a measure of precaution.

Edith Cavell was like a mother to her disguised patients. She nursed them with fanatical devotion until the agent of the organization made his appearance, in order to collect the now convalescent soldiers for the march across the frontier.

The crossing of the frontier was organized as follows: In the first place, groups of five or six men were formed, and to each a guide was allotted. This guide was perfectly acquainted with the country on either side of the frontier. Each man was given a false pass, in the name of some local Belgian authority, to the effect that he was an inhabitant of some village on the Dutch frontier. He was further provided with a document, signed by a municipal officer, from which it appeared that he was a craftsman of some kind, who was now returning home, either because his work was finished, or because the war had made it impossible to continue it. To complete these documents the fugitive was also given a skilfully forged order, signed by one of the German military authorities, to the effect that the artisan was to return immediately to his own home. The falsifications of these last documents were constantly improved. In order that no doubt should be entertained as to their genuine character, the holders of such documents were required to return home within a definite time, or the railway journey which they were to make was prescribed. Sometimes the order required the holder to report himself, on his way home, at other military posts, and to see that the day and hour of reporting himself were noted on the document.

In this way many wounded officers and men in the care of Edith Cavell found their way across the Dutch frontier and rejoined the combatant troops. Presently the day arrived when Miss Cavell had sent the last of her convalescent soldiers back to the Army, and she subsequently served the organization in other ways.

At the beginning of the war many enemy soldiers

were lurking behind the German front. They formed themselves into companies; they were still armed, and had no intention of surrendering to the German troops. These companies hid in the forests and hilly districts; they lived on game, and such food as the countryfolk brought them by night. The number of these fugitives in the rear of the army was considerable. In some places the leaders of these companies contrived to hold out as late as June, 1915. As a matter of course, they inflicted such damage as they could on the enemy. The author still remembers with a slight shudder an incident in which he himself was concerned. It was in 1915, and he was resting with his company in the district lying between the Argonne and the small French town of Dun. With a comrade he was walking through the moonlit night; a long way from the rest billets, or from any German troops, and a long way behind the front, in the neighbourhood of the village of Montigny, being in fact on the way thither. There had been some talk of shooting a wild boar that night. A narrow path wound into the forest; so steep that neither of us had breath to spare for speech. The path led us to the edge of a meadow, which lay at a lower level; suddenly we turned a corner into a forest ride, and stood still, in sudden alarm. About a hundred yards distant, in marching order, rifle on shoulder, a body of French soldiers were approaching us over the soft woodland soil. There seemed to be about a hundred of them, and their officers were marching at the head of the column. As we caught sight of the French, and the

French caught sight of us, both parties stood still for some moments. The French may have supposed that a whole company was marching up behind us. But since this was not the case, the two of us closed the incident by taking one leap into the wood, scrambling down a few declivities, still under cover of the wood, rushing back to our billets, and giving the alarm. It was not until a month later that a whole battalion, which was still holding out in this hilly district, was rounded up and taken prisoner.

The soldiers whom the organization now began to send to Edith Cavell may perhaps have come from such formations. It was her business to harbour these men in Brussels until they could be sent over the frontier.

Just as the organization was beginning, on an extensive scale, to withdraw these unwounded soldiers from Belgium, the German authorities got wind of its existence. It was a series of accidents that led to its discovery. The fact that strange men were often seen in Miss Cavell's house was the first circumstance to arouse suspicion. The police and the counter-espionage agents began to observe the house, and their suspicions were confirmed by their observations. The authorities did not move at once; they continued to watch the house, hoping to catch the individual accomplices in the act. As a matter of fact, this was not particularly difficult; the transactions of the organization were becoming more and more obvious, more and more incautious, and it needed no great ingenuity to break the net and expose its methods.

In the spring of 1915, when the organization had been nine months at work, the counter-espionage service intervened. Edith Cavell and a large number of the members of the organization were arrested. All the accused, including Edith Cavell, confessed to their activities, so that the whole matter was handed over to the Military Court. The Court proceeded to indict the prisoners "in respect of the case of Phillippe Baucq and others," since the Belgian, Phillippe Baucq, was regarded as the chief offender. When the trial opened Edith Cavell sat in the midst of a numerous group of prisoners, all of whom were charged with military conspiracy. The prosecution was represented by Kriegsgerichtsrat Stöber; the Court consisted of German officers; and the counsel for the defence were the Brussels advocates, Sadi Kirschen and Thomas Braun. After the indictment had been read Edith Cavell was called, and her interrogation began. This interrogation, which was recorded by her advocate, and subsequently published in the *Echo de Paris*, began as follows:

"Edith Cavell declared that she was forty-nine years of age, and a British subject.

THE JUDGE: Between November, 1914, and July, 1915, you harboured French and English soldiers, among them a colonel, all being in civilian clothing. You have assisted Belgians, Frenchmen and Englishmen to return to military service at the front. You have supported them and have given them money.

EDITH CAVELL: I have.

THE JUDGE: With whom were you associated in carrying out these transactions?

CAVELL: With Monsieur Capian, Mademoiselle Martin, and Messieurs Derveau and Libiez.

JUDGE: Who was the head, the creator of the organization?

CAVELL: There was no head.

JUDGE: Was not the Prince de Croy the head of it?

CAVELL: No, the Prince de Croy confined himself to sending us men whom he had helped with money.

JUDGE: Why have you committed the actions of which you are accused?

To this Edith Cavell answered at some length, stating that she had believed that all the men whom she had helped to cross the frontier were in danger of their lives. This was her whole defence, her whole justification."

Edith Cavell, like the majority of the accused, was sentenced to death. Since it was evident that she had never at any time acted from avaricious or otherwise morally reprehensible motives, the opinion was immediately expressed in Germany, even by officers of high rank, that the sentence of death should be commuted to one of imprisonment. By military law the supreme instance of the Military Court was the general commanding the Army. He confirmed the verdict. The Governor-General of Belgium, the Freiherr von Bissing, did not countersign the death-warrant of the English nurse. It is positively known to-day that the

political department of the German Government General, of which the Freiherr von Bissing was the head,
did everything humanly possible to avert the execution
of the death-sentence.

The Freiherr von Bissing, a man whose noble and
chivalrous character has always been recognized even
by the enemy, did his utmost, but his efforts were unavailing. Edith Cavell was shot. The statement which
was current in the whole of the enemy press, during
and after the war, and was recently revived in an
English film, to the effect that the execution was carried out in a horrible manner, is absolutely false.
Edith Cavell was bound to a post; and the officer's
word of command had not died away before the bullets
of the German soldiers had killed her on the spot.

How seriously detrimental to the success of the German troops the activities of Nurse Cavell must have
been is shown by a very conclusive document. Lord
Bryce has published his war speeches and articles in
volume form. The book was reviewed by Robert Arch
in *Justice* (30th January, 1919). What the reviewer
says of the fate of Edith Cavell is all the more signifi-
cant in that his review is, on the whole, animated by a
spirit which is anything but friendly to Germany. He
says:

"Lord Bryce, and others also, would have done well
to refrain from exploiting such incidents as the execution of Miss Cavell. What Miss Cavell did was
unquestionably deserving of capital punishment in ac-

cordance with the laws of war. The privilege of sex in such matters was recognized neither by our allies nor by our enemies, and it is time that we recognized this, and admitted that Miss Cavell heroically ventured her life and died for her country, but that she was no more and no less 'murdered' than thousands of men who fell in honourable fight on the field of battle."

CHAPTER TWELVE

AFTER THE WAR

WHEN the Armistice in the forest of Compiègne put an end to the conflict of the central European nations, the guns were still thundering in some parts of Europe. In Russia the White armies were fighting desperately against the Soviets, and in this conflict espionage played a very active part. The Russians who had instituted the Bolshevik dictatorship had at their disposal numbers of highly intelligent men, inspired with enthusiasm for the new State, who were ready to undertake the dangerous duties of the spy. The history of the secret service, with whose assistance the Russian authorities shattered the White armies, is the history of a savage and fanatical espionage on the part of Reds and Whites alike. It is a history that is full of instances of horrible cruelty, of atrocities committed by both sides alike when a spy was captured.

In the year 1929 Orloff, a Councillor of State, was accused, in Berlin, of forging political documents. The evidence proved his guilt, and he was condemned to a term of imprisonment. This man was deeply involved in all the important undertakings of the Russian secret service after the war.

While his trial was proceeding there was suddenly an outburst of indignation in the whole of the German press, for during the course of the trial the most amazing revelations had been made. It was proved that quite a number of highly-placed German officials maintained their own secret service bureaux, to which they paid large sums of money, and whose duties were varied and peculiar. In addition to obtaining information of the political intentions of foreign countries, these bureaux were very largely concerned with the internal politics of Germany. The press suddenly realized that everyone and everything in Germany was spied upon by the agents of these bureaux, and it finally emerged that these governmental authorities were actually spying upon one another. It was a singular fact that nearly all the directors of such bureaux were Russians, who, though some of them were naturalized, employed hardly any but Russians. The facts that were elicited during the course of this trial are typical of espionage as it exists to-day. In all European countries, apart from Russia, where the political situation is fundamentally different from that of other countries, political espionage, applied to domestic affairs, is to-day an activity which is subventioned by the State.

Generally speaking, in all European countries there is to-day, twelve years after the war, far more espionage than there was before the war. To-day the Governments of all countries have established organizations which inform them, with astonishing promptitude, of any change in the political conditions of their own country. This promptitude, however, is seldom coupled with reliability.

The leaders of the great parties are kept under observation. The Opposition is watched and spied upon, and even members of the Ministry who belong to the Opposition parties are similarly watched. In order to defeat his political opponents Mussolini has covered the whole of Italy with a monstrous network of secret agents. Primo de Rivera had his spies principally in the Army, which constituted a danger to his dictatorship. England and France are spending enormous sums in ascertaining the intentions of the Communists, and in Germany, as was shown in the Orloff trial, the same conditions obtain.

It is worth while to consider this Orloff a little more closely. It is worth while because here we have a man who has really been a spy all his life. Needless to say, the Councillor Orloff rarely took an active part in acts of espionage. His place was in the central bureau, but all the threads of the secret service were gathered into his hands. The son of middle-class parents, he studied the law, entered the service of the Government, and took part, as an officer of the reserve, in the Russo-Japanese campaign. From 1906 to 1917 he was an examining magistrate in St. Petersburg, and earned promotion by his skill in handling an important case of forgery. He now became Public Prosecutor, and Councillor of State, and an "Excellency," and was finally appointed examining judge of the secret department of the political police. Of these examining judges, whose position, under the Tsarist Government, was one of supreme political importance, there were only five or six in the whole of Russia. Such judges even took precedence of the Public Prosecutor in their particular Governments, as did Orloff in St. Petersburg. With his appointment to this office he entered upon a sinister career, which rose to the highest summits and sank to the lowest depths of human existence.

Armed with almost absolute power, Orloff travelled all over Russia, as the head of a vast organization whose task it was to keep under observation the Socialist and Communist leaders. Lenin, Trotsky, and many another Communist whose name has since become famous, was arrested at the instance of Orloff, and condemned to imprisonment, or transportation, or death. Every political conspiracy that was detected by the secret police was subjected to this man's investigations. In the days of the Tsarist Government hundreds of conspirators were condemned by Orloff to face a firing-party, and thousands upon thousands were transported to Siberia. His success was due to his ingeniously organized system of political espionage.

In the year 1917 the Russian revolution broke out, and the first thing the new rulers of Russia did was to set a high price on the head of the man who had destroyed so many of their comrades in the days of the Tsar. Orloff fled before he could be arrested, but he found time to take with him all the political records in his archives.

For a time he wandered about Russia in disguise,

having made himself almost unrecognizable by altering
the fashion of his hair and beard, until he at last succeeded in joining one of the White armies. Its leaders
received him with open arms, and he unmasked, in
capacity of a councillor of the supreme military tribunal
of this army, the Bolshevik spies who had been sent
thither by Moscow. Once again he sent hundreds of
men to their deaths; but the mutual hatred of the
parties was now so intense that the spies were no longer
shot, but put to death by torture. Orloff left the White
Army at the instance of its generals. They begged
him to venture into the camp of the enemy; firstly,
in order to assist the imprisoned counter-revolutionaries,
and secondly, in order to spy on the Bolsheviks. And
he had yet a third task to perform: since the White
generals were proposing to strike a blow against Moscow
and Leningrad, Orloff was to recruit men in these cities
who would support the developing attack by an armed
rising in the enemy's capitals.

Orloff prepared himself a passport in the name of
Orlinski, and at the end of 1918 he appeared in Leningrad. He succeeded in obtaining a post as prison
warder. The prisoners in his charge were counter-
revolutionaries. The prison warder, whom no one
recognized, proved his mettle. By listening to private
conversations he was able to connect what he had heard
with actual occurrences, and the Tcheka soon became
aware of his value. Once he was given the task of
obtaining certain information he rose with amazing
rapidity. He became a member of the Tcheka, and

its expert in respect of political offences. In this position he got into touch with the German Intelligence Service, and provided it with valuable material relating to the Russian plans for fomenting a revolution in Germany. Suddenly he disappeared from Leningrad, and, returning to the White armies, became a sort of military attorney-general in the headquarters of Denikin and Wrangel. Once more he was both a spy and a prosecutor, and sent many a man to his death.

But no one in the headquarters of the White Army knew that Orloff-Orlinski, as a member of the Tcheka, had been responsible for the death of many counter-revolutionaries.

When the White armies collapsed, Orloff escaped to London. He became a cook in the Russian Embassy, but no one in the Embassy was aware of his identity. Even while in this position he ferreted out the secrets of the Embassy as far as he was able to do so. He then suddenly left London for Paris, and there, as a spy, he did what he could to the detriment of the Soviet. He was then one of the intimate hangers-on of the late Grand Duke Nicholas.

From Paris he proceeded to Berlin, and there, as an expert in Russian affairs, he found employment with many of the secret intelligence bureaux which enabled the various authorities to spy on one another. But in the end these bureaux wanted more of him than he could give them. They asked for original documents which would afford evidence of the purposes of the Russian Foreign Office; and these were difficult to procure. The demand exceeded the supply, and finally Orloff began to forge documents. The authorities were at first deceived, but when Orloff went so far as to offer such papers to an American journalist he was unmasked.

A deplorable chapter in the history of recent espionage is that which deals with the attitude of the French military authorities towards a disarmed and defeated country. Still more deplorable is the fact that the French secret service had no difficulty in obtaining information as to the military resources of Germany, since an enormous number of Germans were willing, for a small remuneration, to spy on their own country.

This chapter of recent espionage was made public during the trial in the German courts, of the French officer, Captain d'Armont. In the course of this trial the facts were elicited which are related in the following chapter.

CHAPTER THIRTEEN

ARRESTED TWO YARDS FROM THE FRONTIER

IN accordance with the Treaty of Versailles, the German Army destroyed its armaments and munitions of war. An Entente Commission of Control proceeded to Berlin, and, again in accordance with the Treaty, was given the exhaustive list of all the material of war still existing in Germany. The Commission had to be informed precisely where such material was to be found. Its activities were comprehensive, and most of the work was done by its French members, and of these the busiest was Captain Hamaus. This officer organized an extensive system of espionage in Germany, whose purpose was to scent out concealed weapons, if such existed. This system of espionage was very simple, and its success was disgraceful to Germany. Any German who offered to betray concealed war material to this officer was given a contract which assured him of ten per cent. of the current value of the impounded material. Hundreds of Germans approached Captain Hamaus. An Englishman, formerly a staff officer, Captain Vivian Stranders, who was likewise a member of the Commission, contributed to Scherl's *Nachtausgabe*, in May, 1920, an account of the activities of this Frenchman and his comrades. Of particular interest is the passage in which he speaks of "fictitious declarations."

"Through experienced and reliable spies the intelligence officer received not only information as to material unlawfully purchased by agents, but also fictitious declarations, which were intended to obtain, for the officers of the control, access to works whose industrial and technical secrets were of interest to manufacturers of the Entente countries. As chief interpreter I was aware of all such visits, and also of the wording of the denunciations in question. Not in one single case, however, have I been able to discover that any concealed material was ever found in the works visited; and by the very wording of the denunciations, which I had to translate for the other officers, I could always tell that they were fictitious."

Captain Stranders further stated that the French officers constantly had the other Entente officers, who had a more honourable conception of their duties, spied upon by their agents. There was, the Englishman says, "a Polish employée in the central telephone bureau of the Commission. This lady had to supply the intelligence officer (Captain Hamaus) with a confidential report upon all the telephone messages transmitted during the day."

Apparently the French were so apprehensive lest Germany, in spite of her having been disarmed, might in the near future resuscitate her armies, that an extraordinary number of spies were sent out or controlled by the central bureau of the French Intelligence Service in Paris. In the zone of occupation they could, of course, obtain all the information they desired, and it need hardly be said that they were very active in ferreting out the technical secrets of the German chemical factories and other works.

The Paris bureau of the Intelligence Service worked on the same lines as those which it had followed in the years before the war. As then, the central bureau of the service was situated in the Rue François. It had learned much during the war, and above all it had decided to profit by the example of Captain Peeka's school for spies, which had more than once been visited by French officers. A school was established in Aix, in the Villa Lüttitz, a large mansion which had been commandeered by the garrison of occupation. In Germany itself men were recruited for the French Intelligence Service, and these men, before they were sent to spy on their own countrymen, were trained for their task in the Villa Lüttitz. The period of training varied in individual cases; it might be a matter of weeks or even of months. According to their intelligence and fitness for the work, the agents trained in this school were given a definite rank or grade. It is worth while to consider the designations of these grades, for they have in the meantime been generally adopted by the French Intelligence Service, and they enable us to realize the full extent of French espionage in Germany after the war.

The first and lowest grade is that of *dupeur*. He has to profess certain political opinions, to smuggle himself into one of the great German labour organizations, and report as to the intentions of the labour movement. The second grade is that of the *mouton*. The *mouton* is a man whose principal task is to obtain employment in one of the great industrial centres of Germany and ferret out industrial secrets. The third grade is that of *racolleur*. The agent of this grade has to recruit fresh agents by means of money and promises. Nearly all the agents of this class are women. Next comes the *agent baladeur*, who must always be at the disposal of the French Intelligence Service, and is sent from place to place to inquire into individual occurrences. Then comes the *agent fixe*, who lives in a particular German city, and has to send periodical reports of any matters worthy of attention. The highest grade is that of *trafiquant*; and the agent of this grade is always on the move, obtaining plans and documentary details of important political, military and industrial transactions.

In accordance with a long-established tradition, these agents, when they wished to communicate the information which they had secured in Germany, did not forward it direct to Paris, but to an intermediate bureau in a neutral country. This was the French intelligence bureau in Basle, which had branches in Zürich and Berne. The agents, having completed their training, were directed to this bureau, which then dispatched them to Germany, and it was with the Basle bureau that they kept in touch. The head of the bureau, one of the principal agents of the French espionage in Germany, was Captain Pendarie d'Armont, an officer of the French General Staff.

This officer, who was indefatigable in his pursuit of information, had organized subordinate bureaux in the towns of the occupied area of the Rhineland, and these were instructed to recruit agents of their own. Above all, they endeavoured to suborn relatives of men serving in the German Army, so that they might entice these soldiers into their net. Of these smaller bureaux the most active was that established in Mainz, and directed by the French lieutenant Thomas. This bureau indulged in wholesale methods of espionage. We know of one case in which it adopted an absolutely grotesque expedient for attaining its ends. Having obtained a divisional Army List, the bureau sent letters to a large number of non-commissioned officers. One of these epistles, each of which contained notes for three hundred marks, and almost all of which (but not quite all) were given by the recipients of their commanding officers, is here reproduced. It was addressed to "Herr Eischelser, Unteroffizier, Meiningen, Infanterie—Regiment 14, Grenadierkaserne." The text is as follows:

"HONOURED SIR!

"Since I have learned from friends of mine that you would be willing to assist us in respect of our aims, I hereby inform you that I am in a position to make you an advantageous offer. It would, however, be neces-

sary for you to call on me here in Mainz before we could come to a final understanding. Hoping that I may soon see you here, and with Communistic greetings,
"THOMAS."

The address given at the foot of this letter was: "Herr Thomas, Mainz 2. Heiliggrabgasse, Block 1. Door on the left. 1st floor."

And the letter contained a postscript:

"P.S.—Herewith I send the money for your travelling expenses."

The "Communistic greetings," and the enclosure of a sum of money far in excess of the railway fare, were doubtless regarded by Monsieur Thomas as touches of ingenious *finesse*.

The German authorities, and in particular the Reichswehrministerium, began to be aware of the activities of Captain d'Armont in May, 1921. At that time the captain called himself Weingärtner, and the Mainz bureau had acquired the services of several soldiers of the German Reichswehr, who betrayed such military secrets as were known to them. They imparted their information to "Captain Weingärtner" in person, meeting him in the neighbourhood of the German-Swiss frontier. D'Armont had a number of such spies working for him.

To begin with, there was a man by the name of Binz, who busied himself with making the acquaintance of soldiers of the Würtemberg regiments, and asking them questions. Binz actually had written instructions from Weingärtner, which required him, amongst other things, to get hold of certain secret orders of the military authorities, which were definitely designated by their numbers. These orders were filed in the offices of the Reichswehr in Stuttgart, and by means of false keys and pick-locks he broke into the offices at night. Binz obtained assistance from a lance-corporal of the Reichswehr, one Bornemann. Another of Captain d'Armont's principal agents was Rudolf Senftele of Lörrach, in Baden, who observed the manœuvres of the Reichswehr, and above all the rifle-practice of the troops on the Grafenwöhr range. Senftele also recruited one Retzner, a soldier of the Reichswehr, and introduced him to d'Armont. Retzner was instructed to report from time to time on the spirit of the ranks of the Reichswehr. Around these men was a whole network of spies of varying importance, whose task it was to spy upon the German Reichswehr.

But one day the German police got wind of these spies. A letter from Captain Weingärtner to Binz fell into the hands of the authorities. The whole company of spies was silently watched, and then suddenly arrested. It was known that the head of this organization was Captain d'Armont, who was out of reach in Basle.

Then, one day, an official of the postal censorship in Constance noticed a letter addressed to an Ensign Knall, who was supposed to be serving in a battalion stationed in Constance. But since there was no ensign of this name in Constance the letter could not be delivered, and remained lying in the post office. The envelope felt as though it contained money, and the official decided to open it. He found in it a Swiss twenty-franc note, and a letter from Herr Weingärtner to the ensign, in which the soldier was invited to meet Herr Weingärtner one day not far from the German-Swiss frontier, as the writer had something of importance to say to him. The twenty-franc note was enclosed to cover his travelling expenses.

The postal official, to whom this letter seemed to be of a suspicious nature, forwarded it to the political police in Constance. The police commissary Woeger, an expert in matters of espionage, realized at once what was afoot, and he resolved that Captain d'Armont should be made to pay for spying on Germany. Since no Ensign Knall existed, the commissary decided that he himself would act the part of the soldier. He accordingly sent Herr Weingärtner a polite little note, thanking him for his enclosure, and declaring that he would be very willing to meet him. But the ensign had his own ideas regarding the place where they should meet. He wished the interview to take place in the village of Kreuzlingen, close to the Swiss frontier. The ensign's note was promptly answered. Weingärtner agreed to the time and place mentioned, and the two men met as agreed. They had a long conversation, and Herr Weingärtner was delighted to find that the ensign had no serious objection to undertaking a little espionage. Indeed, the soldier told him then and there something that was quite new to him, and as a reward, and to encourage him to further efforts, Weingärtner gave him fifty Swiss francs. They then parted, having agreed to meet again some little time later.

This time the rendezvous was near the village of Arlem, once more close to the frontier. For this second meeting the commissary had made the most efficient preparations. The German frontier guards were sent elsewhere, so that Captain d'Armont should see nothing to arouse his suspicions. But close to the frontier two peasants were working in the fields. They were detectives, disguised by von Woeger.

D'Armont appeared punctually at the appointed hour. He stood on the frontier, not far from a Swiss frontier guard. Ensign Knall was likewise punctual. He waved his hand to the captain, who crossed the frontier into German territory, and approached him. Ten yards from the frontier he stopped, and waited for Knall. The ensign came forward, and shook hands with the captain; and the latter, who that day, for some reason, felt very insecure on German territory, proposed at once that they should cross the Swiss frontier and go to a certain tavern. Knall, however, suggested that they should go a little farther in the opposite direction. But suddenly d'Armont turned, looked uneasily about him, and made a step towards the frontier. Instantly the peasants threw down their tools.

They ran like the wind at the Frenchman. The ensign dropped his mask, seizing d'Armont by the arm; but the captain wrenched himself free. The detectives, in their peasant clothing, flung themselves on him; he defended himself desperately, striking out and struggling like a trapped animal; but some two yards from the frontier the detectives overpowered him, pulled him to the ground, and handcuffed him.

He was searched on the spot, and on his person was found a list of his principal agents in Germany, whose arrest was ordered by telegraph that very day.

The captain was brought up for trial in March, 1924. Three Stuttgart advocates defended him, and during the early stages of the trial he absolutely refused to give any information as to his identity and his activities. The witnesses in the case were the arrested agents, who had already been tried and sentenced to long terms of imprisonment.

D'Armont could no longer deny the nature and extent of his activities; so he declared that Woeger had seized him on Swiss territory, and that his arrest was consequently illegal, and an infraction of international law. The President of the Court, however, who was also the President of the Senate, Richter, read a declaration of the Swiss Government to the effect that the arrest had indubitably been made on German territory, at a point rather more than two yards from the frontier.

When d'Armont saw that his assertion was unavailing, he declared that the commissary had enticed him on to German territory. To this the President replied that, after all, Germany still had the right to defend herself against foreign espionage. The Attorney-General, Ebermayer, described the accused as the director-in-chief of the French espionage against Germany. He had employed twenty-six agents, and his activities had been in the highest degree detrimental to the German Empire. It was true that d'Armont had only done his duty as a servant of his Government; nevertheless, a plea of mitigating circumstances could not be allowed. His German agents, who betrayed their Fatherland for a little easily-earned money, were the worst of traitors. The accused was an officer who had acted as a spy in the service of his country, so that he had not acted dishonourably, since an officer who performs such services for his country is not dishonoured thereby. Nevertheless, the French courts had sentenced German officers who were similarly employed to immoderately long terms of imprisonment. Still, no German court would ever think of taking reprisal for such sentences. At the same time, they were dealing with a flagrant breach of international law, which called for an exemplary penalty.

The French spy was sentenced to twelve years' imprisonment. In passing sentence the Court declared that d'Armont had inflicted serious injury on Germany. Germany was completely disarmed and all but powerless; but among the few powers that remained to it was that of keeping its armed forces in a state of preparedness and efficiency, in order that they might preserve the peace and maintain order in the interior of the Empire. The German Empire must needs defend itself when the discipline of the Army was jeopardized by inducing its soldiers to act as spies on their own country.

The apprehension of d'Armont was a serious blow to the French authorities, who had lost in him one of their most valuable spies. In violation of the spirit of international law, they threatened to proceed to reprisals in the occupied zone unless Captain d'Armont was released. And although it had been clearly proved that the captain was a spy, although, as a French officer, he had crossed the German frontier in pursuance of activities of a hostile nature, the French carried out their threats. In Düsseldorf they arrested the President of the Senate, Dr. Lenzberg, a Judge of the Supreme Court, and since they were obliged to release him, as he was seriously ill, they arrested the Essen Public Prosecutor, Schutze-Pellkum, the President of the Supreme Court in Bochum, and the Burgomaster of Gelsenkirchen, Wedelstädt.

It was a long time before they released these three men, who had been arrested as hostages. Subsequently, Captain d'Armont was pardoned and expelled from Germany.

CHAPTER FOURTEEN

MARTHE MOREUIL: ESPIONAGE BY PARACHUTE

IN the year 1920 an instance of espionage was discovered in Paris which evoked an unprecedented outburst of indignation in the French press, and indeed throughout the country, since it was assumed that the persons apprehended—a woman and three men —were German spies. The indignation was somewhat allayed by the fact that the spies proved to be not German, but English agents, who had been spying out the military secrets of a friendly nation for the British Government. The indignation was succeeded by surprise and consternation; there was something like a diplomatic quarrel between the two friendly Powers; and then the whole affair was suppressed, in the interest of the friendly relations existing between the two countries, which had, of course, been somewhat disturbed by the incident. The principal aim of English espionage in France had been to acquire information concerning the French air forces, and as the matter had to be suppressed, since it might otherwise have had serious political consequences, the French Government inspired the statement that the whole affair was "more gossip than truth, a farce rather than a tragedy."

The truth of the matter, however, which was a highly

unpleasant affair for the authorities concerned, was as follows:

In a small French town there was living, after the war, a frugal and respectable official, whose wife and children made excessive demands on his modest income. He was, however, a strict and authoritative father. The name of the official was Moreuil. He had a daughter, Marthe Moreuil, who caused him a great deal of anxiety. As she grew older his anxiety increased; she was a strikingly beautiful girl, with a light, supple figure. The narrow and monotonous existence imposed upon the family by the father did not please the girl at all; she was fond of life, and the veto placed upon her harmless pleasures had, in the end, an unfortunate effect upon her character; she became irritable and unduly emotional. By the time she was fifteen years of age she had had enough of her parents' house. Somehow she must escape from this atmosphere of eternal boredom. Since she was perfectly well aware that her father would never release her from his control, she conceived of a grotesque expedient. She expressed the desire to enter a convent; she had resolved to become a nun; and all of a sudden she became excessively pious. In the end she persuaded her father to send her to a convent school; and M. Moreuil presently consented, since it seemed the best thing to do with a girl who had caused him so much anxiety. And accordingly, Marthe Moreuil was sent to a convent school. For three days all went well; then she ran away to Paris.

What can a young and pretty girl do in Paris if she has no money, and wishes to avoid the hard work and the subordinate position of a domestic servant? She can become an artist's model.

Marthe Moreuil became an artist's model. She wrote to her parents informing them that she had adopted the career of an artist, but the father, who was excessively sceptical of his daughter's qualifications for such a career, went to Paris to bring her home, only to find that she had left the address from which she had written. Marthe Moreuil had, as a matter of fact, left Paris in the company of two painters, to whom she did actually sit from time to time; then she wandered all over France, and her father finally gave up trying to find her; especially as her family received, from time to time, picture post-cards from all parts of the country, which showed that she was still alive, and presumably well. This life suited Marthe excellently, until it began to be rumoured among the painters of Paris that the model Moreuil was possessed of a peculiarity which was disturbing and even dangerous. She became attached to her employers; she was a "limpet." Those who had anything to do with her found it extremely difficult to get rid of her; and at last the day came when Marthe Moreuil found herself in serious difficulty, because no one would any longer engage her as a model. She tried all sorts of callings; for a time she was a nurse in the clinic of a Dr. Rabinovitch, in Neuilly, and while at this clinic she informed her parents that she was studying medicine; but she soon tired of the nursing profession, and began to haunt the bars and cafés of the capital. She was sitting one afternoon in a café, when an old gentleman seated himself at her table. He was an aristocratic-looking old gentleman, who wore his hair, which was already grey upon the temples, rather longer than is usual; but the fashion suited him. He seemed to be waiting for something or someone; he looked through the newspapers with a bored and abstracted air, but presently laid them aside. It seemed to Marthe Moreuil that she might help him to pass the time. The two were soon deep in conversation, and the stranger seemed to be so interested in his new acquaintance that Marthe, who was feeling more than a little depressed by her financial difficulties, treated him as a father confessor. She told him her whole story, and when she had finished she declared that she did not know what to do next. In the course of further conversation it appeared that the stranger was a man of strict and definite moral principles. It was his conviction, he said, that everyone should follow a reputable calling, and he asked the girl what kind of work would interest her. Marthe Moreuil did not hesitate; she said that she really felt that she had in her the makings of a great actress, and she wished she could find some means of coming before the public. The old gentleman thought that he might be able to help her in this connection, and he made an appointment to meet her, in the café, on the following day. At their second interview he suggested to her that she might make her living as a parachute artiste. Ten years ago such a calling was still regarded as extremely hazardous, and was, therefore, well remunerated.

Marthe Moreuil accepted his proposal, and during the next few weeks she saw a great deal of the old gentleman. He took her to fashionable resorts which hitherto she had known only from the outside, and finally he told her frankly that in the calling which she was about to adopt it was possible to earn such large sums of money that she would from now onwards be able to live a life that would call for a luxurious setting. Marthe now asked him to explain his meaning more exactly. She learned that her new friend was a man of versatile qualifications and interests, and that he was especially interested in the numbers of the French aeroplanes, the strength and composition of the individual squadrons, the capacity and position of the aerodromes, and above all, the wireless stations which were able to keep in touch with aeroplanes. It was not difficult to persuade Marthe Moreuil to fall in with her friend's proposals. She now became an "artiste"; she was given a very safe and reliable parachute, which had been imported from England. One day a private aeroplane was engaged, and then came the moment when Marthe Moreuil took her first leap from an aeroplane in flight. After the pilot had been cruising for perhaps half an hour round the point selected for her descent, during which time the girl gradually mastered her fear, she leapt into the air and came safely to ground. She made dozens of such descents in the course of the next week, until she had lost all fear.

She then sent her parents a picture post-card, on which she informed them that she had become an aviator.

After this her duties became more serious. The old gentleman, who had never told her his name, now found her a place in the establishment of a dealer in wireless apparatus in the Rue de Surenne, near the Madeleine. One morning, when Marthe Moreuil entered the shop, she found her friend in the company of two other men. This shop was rather a curious establishment. There was a big show-room, in which a large number of wireless sets were on view, and behind it were offices, with a number of conference-rooms, whose walls were carefully padded. It appeared later that these men were Englishmen.

The name of Marthe Moreuil's friend was William Fisher. He was a Pole, naturalized in England, and an agent of the English Intelligence Service. The head of the business was a Mr. Henry Leather. He described himself as an engineer, but was actually an officer on the active list of the British Army. The third man was Oliver Phillips, a non-commissioned officer of the British Army. Leather was the director of the firm, Phillips the book-keeper, and William Fisher the packer. Despite the difference in the social positon of these three men, they were all equally well dressed, and were evidently on terms of intimacy.

That morning Marthe Moreuil was told the plain truth. Her employers were prepared to pay her a monthly salary of one thousand two hundred francs, and all expenses, if she would visit all the aerodromes of France, in the guise of a parachutist, in order to secure such information as she might be instructed to obtain. She was provided with certain cameras of excellent quality, which she was to take with her on her travels, and she was given a few test commissions, which she fulfilled to the satisfaction of her employers. When it came to ascertaining the strength of the air service, or other military secrets, she resorted to the time-honoured methods of all female spies; she became intimate with a number of flying officers, spent the night in their quarters, and stole such books, orders and other official documents as she could lay her hands on. She brought the stolen material to the wireless dealer's, and was paid for her services.

At St. Nazaire the Army was about to test a new hydroplane. Marthe Moreuil went thither and photographed what there was to photograph. Then she was sent to Bordeaux, to learn where the stocks of benzine and lubricating oil were situated. At an aviation meeting at Bordeaux she gave her usual performance with the parachute, and behind the back of her unsuspecting pilot she photographed the mooring-place of the military hydroplanes. In the same way she photographed the aerodromes of Guery, Hyères and St. Raphael. She concealed her camera in the lining of her cloak. In order to arouse no suspicion, she did not continue to return to Paris, but spent much of her time in the boarding-houses of small watering-places, and received her instructions by post. It was "Mr. Leather" who gave her these instructions. He sent her envelopes which contained only blank sheets of paper. If these were brushed over with a certain liquid, the writing on them became visible.

Marthe Moreuil, on the French Riviera, received such a letter by express post, and when she had read it she realized that she was in danger, that her friends of the wireless shop were under observation as persons suspected of espionage, and that she too had attracted the attention of the authorities. She immediately left the Riviera. She hoped to escape by proceeding to Paris, and then to Calais, and crossing to Dover. In any case she must try to get into touch with her employers, in order to obtain more money, for at the moment she possessed only the price of her ticket to Paris. She entered the train, and having managed to obtain a compartment to herself, she opened her portmanteau, went through her letters and papers in order to remove anything that might arouse suspicion, tore the documents into fragments, and threw them out of the window shortly before the train reached Avignon. A few minutes later these scraps of paper were found by a railway employé, who hurried to the nearest station with them, for he realized that the torn documents related to military matters, of which he had some knowledge, as he had been a sergeant during the war. In the railway station, as luck would have it, were a number of French officers. The railway employé went eagerly up to them and reported his find; and by chance one of the officers present was attached to the French Intelligence Service. This officer knew that a Marthe Moreuil was suspected of espionage; and among the torn papers he found a hotel bill which bore this woman's name; he saw, too, that the scraps of papers were fragments of secret military orders; he ran to the nearest telephone and warned the Intelligence Service in Paris, and as Marthe Moreuil alighted from the train she was arrested. She gave the police no trouble of any sort. She confessed to everything immediately, and gave the names and described the transactions of her accomplices. The officer who was interrogating her shook his head; he had never yet encountered a spy of this kind, one who positively insisted on betraying her accomplices. When she had told him everything she was removed into custody, and the prison doctor, who examined her immediately, called up the officer in charge of the case the same evening, and informed him that he had arrested an extraordinarily hysterical patient. Marthe Moreuil, however, asked for pen and paper, and wrote to her parents, informing them that she was now engaged in politics, and had been placed under temporary arrest because she had thwarted the plans of an eminent politician.

The three Englishmen whom Marthe Moreuil had named were at once arrested. Their premises were searched, but not a single incriminating document was discovered. The French Intelligence Service sent an agent to London, who soon succeeded in ascertaining that of the three men arrested two were soldiers on the active list, while one was a secret agent. It was further ascertained that the business which had enabled the three Englishmen, and a lady secretary, who was given quite extraordinary liberty, to live in a very good style, had earned about three hundred francs monthly. But the evidence most damaging to the Englishmen was given by a certain barkeeper. This man deposed that the director of the wireless business, Leather, had his letters sent not to the shop but to the bar. There was a whole list of names in which letters were addressed to the bar, and all these letters were taken away by Leather. The three Englishmen confessed to nothing; they denied emphatically that they had been guilty of espionage, and they only confessed that they were, respectively, officers of the British Army and an agent of the Intelligence Service when it was no longer possible for them to dispute the facts.

It was decided, since the affair was equally painful to both the Governments concerned, that it had better be forgotten. The only person who made it difficult to follow this course was Marthe Moreuil. She was possessed by an absolutely fanatical desire to confess her exploits, and filled whole volumes with her depositions. Once, in the course of her examination, as she was being led through the forecourt of the Palais de Justice, she passed the reporters of the Parisian newspapers, who were following the proceedings. When Marthe Moreuil realized that they were newspaper men she drew herself up to her full height, and called out to them:

"Write as little as you possibly can about my great

case, so that the principals shall not succeed in escaping!"

The whole affair finally became so difficult that it was unobtrusively adjusted. If anyone ever mentioned the case to Victor Hervé that politician uttered only one word: "Shocking!"

When Marthe Moreuil was released from custody she went to the offices of all the Parisian newspapers, and obtained copies of those issues in which there was any mention of her. She then bought, with her last coppers, a large stamped envelope, and posted all these reports of her case to her parents.

(2)

THE END

www.ingramcontent.com/pod-product-compliance
Lightning Source LLC
Chambersburg PA
CBHW020049180626
46812CB00006B/2258